BEN
ARCHER

and
THE ALIEN SKILL

Human or alien?

Rae Knightly

BEN ARCHER AND THE ALIEN SKILL
THE ALIEN SKILL SERIES, BOOK 2
Copyright © 2018 by Rae Knightly.

For information contact :
http://www.raeknightly.com

Cover design by PINTADO
Book Formatting by Derek Murphy @Creativindie
ISBN-13: 978-1722123543
ISBN-10: 1722123540

First Edition: September 2018

CONTENTS

CHAPTER ONE

The Spacecraft

Once more, Inspector James Hao found himself staring at the final report containing the results of the blood sample. No matter how hard he tried to make sense of it, the evidence was undeniable: the individual the sample had been extracted from was not a human being.

Hao couldn't believe that, a little over a month ago, he had been sitting opposite the subject in the interrogation room of the Vancouver Police Department. Never would the Inspector have suspected that, behind the innocent features of a twelve-year-old boy, lay a creature from another planet. Hao's stomach twisted at the thought.

A week ago, High Inspector George Tremblay, Head of the National Aerial Division of the CSIS, had tapped the file with the tips of his fingers. "This file remains between us," he had said, eyeing Hao and his collegue, Connelly. The three men had stood in the High Inspector's office, facing each other.

Tremblay had lifted an eyebrow at Connelly. "You took the sample without my prior authorization. I should fire you for acting in such an unprofessional manner. You can consider yourself lucky that your hunch about the subject was correct. Nevertheless, this information will not enter the official investigation and is not to be mentioned beyond this office. The fact that this child, this Benjamin Archer, is an extraterrestrial must remain between us. Is that clear?"

Hao had observed Connelly out of the corner of his eye, secretly satisfied to watch his colleague being reprimanded by their chief. Even though he had taken a dislike to his colleague and had personnally disapproved of the blood extraction, he had to hand it to Connelly for getting results. All in all, he had to admit that Connelly's methods of investigation were particularly efficient if not particularly legal.

The cell phone on Hao's desk buzzed, pulling him out of his thoughts, causing him to start. A message arrived, accompanied by a tiny image. Hao's forehead–creased in concentration a second ago–softened, and a chuckle escaped his lips. He pressed the image to enlarge it, and the huge, black nuzzle of an English Shephard appeared. The black dog was checking out the camera of whoever was taking the picture.

The message read: DID YOU FORGET ME?

Hao smiled and checked his watch. It was close to midnight at the Dugout, located in Eastern Canada, which meant it was nine pm where the message had originated.

What am I doing, still stuck at my desk at this hour? Hao brooded.

He hesitated for an instant, then pressed on the message to dial the number. The phone rang once before it was picked up, and a woman's voice answered in surprise, "Hello?"

"Hi, Lizzie," Hao said.

"Jimmy?" the woman said. There was shuffling in the background and Hao heard Lizzie's muffled voice, "Still! Sit still, Buddy!" Then her voice sounded clearer. "Oh my gosh! You should see that! He knows it's you! Yes, Buddy! It's your daddy! Your long-lost daddy..."

Hao heard the English Shephard bark happily, and he was reminded people lived normal, tranquil lives out in the real world.

"Jimmy?" Lizzie began. "I can't believe it's you. I sent that picture of Buddy, but never thought you'd actually have time to call back. Must be my lucky day!"

Hao grinned. "How are you, Sis?"

Lizzie sighed in an exaggerated manner. "Do I really need to tell you? Buddy uprooted my rosebushes this afternoon. You know how we love him around here, but, honestly, I love my flowers more."

Hao could hear Buddy panting in the background.

Lizzie continued, "I haven't heard from you in ages! When are you coming home?"

Hao's mood darkened as his eyes slid back to the blood file on his desk. "Not anytime soon. I've got a big case on my hands. Probably the biggest I'll ever work on." He sighed. "I realize Buddy's a burden for you. Do you want me to contact the dog kennel we talked about?"

Lizzie remained silent for a moment, before answering earnestly, "Of course not. I love my roses, but if it helps you, then I'm happy to keep Buddy for a bit longer. You know Geoffrey and I wouldn't want to see him cooped up and miserable."

Hao let out a silent breath of relief. "Thanks. I owe you one. When this is over, we'll go pick out some rose-bushes together."

"You?" Lizzie scoffed. "In a plant nursery? Never gonna happen!"

They both laughed.

"Seriously, Jimmy," Lizzie said with a concerned voice. "There's always a new case popping up. You make it sound as if you were the only one catching the bad guys. I know I'm repeating myself, but bad guys will be around with or without you. And, trust me, there's a dozen younger James Bonds out there longing to take your place."

Hao scoffed, "Take it easy, Sis, I'm not that old!"

Lizzie clicked her tongue which meant to him that she wasn't ready to crack jokes. She pushed on. "If you were still married, your wife would be the one scolding you instead of me. So brace yourself while I nag you for a bit!"

Hao stood with a knowing smile. He paced along the office window overlooking a cavernous hangar and let her have her moment.

"I know how important it is to you to put the criminals behind bars and I, more than anyone, appreciate how hard you work to keep we little citizens safe," Lizzie spoke. "But, you have to stop acting like you're the only one carrying the burden." Her voice sounded thick with worry as she added, "I just want to make sure you stop in time."

While he listened, Hao gazed at the impressive, alien spacecraft that hovered a few feet from the concrete floor at the center of the dim hangar. Everyone, except for security, had left for the night. Only a couple of emergency and forgotten office lights illuminated the area. He thought he saw a movement blend into the shadow cast by the spacecraft and leaned forward, forgetting the phone stuck to his ear.

Lizzie's concerned voice came through to him again. "I know you. You wouldn't call unless something was wrong. Is something the matter?"

Since nothing moved in the grey hangar, except for his own reflection in his office window, Hao's well-built frame relaxed, and he turned to head back to his desk.

"Jimmy? Are you listening?" she asked.

"Hm, yeah, I'm listening," he replied with a tired voice. He sat back in his office chair and rubbed his left temple as he shut his eyes. He needed to rest, but the case wouldn't let him go. And suddenly he realized why.

"It's weird," he said thoughtfully, speaking more to himself than his sister. "You know me: you know I'm an expert at telling good from bad, right? I mean, I understand the mind of a murderer; I know how to pick out a crook; I'm always a step ahead of elaborate thieves. I catch them and put them behind bars, where they belong." He broke off, picking up the file in front of him. "But these ones, Lizzie? Jeez, for all I know, they could start World War Three tomorrow, and I wouldn't even see it coming." He shook his head, surprised at his own confession. "The thing is, for the first time in my career, I've been asked to chase down criminals I don't understand." He paused. "And that frightens me."

Agent Theodore Edmond Connelly paused in the shadow of the spacecraft until Hao disappeared from view. The bald, green-eyed man set his jaw: he had almost gotten caught by Hao as he snuck up to the hovering ship. Had Hao spotted him, it would have led to a load of unnecessary questions, something Connelly could not afford to answer right now.

He grimaced while he waited. As soon as Hao moved away from his office window, Connelly reached out to the sleek ship. At the touch of his fingers, an invisible door opened faster than the eye could see. Connelly jumped inside and the door slid shut silently behind him.

Without delay, the bald man approached the front of the spacecraft where he pulled up hovering screens filled with undecipherable patterns and intricate symbols.

Behind these transparent screens, the ship's large window dominated the concrete hangar. Connelly was not worried about being caught. He knew that, while he could look out, no one could look in. He was safe.

After performing a couple of movements over the screens, he connected to the Dugout surveillance cameras. He made sure that they remained disabled and showed static, then worked remotely to activate them again. His mouth turned into a thin line of concentration.

He checked the time. It had been almost four minutes since he had cut the power to the cameras—thus allowing him safe access to the spacecraft. Way too long! If he didn't turn the system on again soon, security would notice—if they hadn't already.

This was all Hao's fault. What was his colleague doing in his office at this time of night? The man's diligence irritated him.

Sure, it served him well, but he had to constantly be on his toes to avoid Hao's scrutiny from focusing on him. For now, Connelly was satisfied to remain in Hao's shadow. It avoided him having to interact too much with others. Hao did all the talking, while Connelly watched and learned. Yet the man kept on intercepting his own progress. Connelly knew that, should Hao become a burden, he would have to silence the man permanently.

At the moment, though, he had more pressing matters. It only took him half a minute to bring the Dugout cameras back online, yet by the time he was finished, his brow creased in pain.

Connelly stood and staggered backwards into a cubicle to the side of the spacecraft. At a wave of his hand, a stream of energy washed over him in blue surges, and his face began to tremble with unnatural speed. He sagged against the back wall, breathing heavily, unable to stop the transformation from taking its course.

Out of his bald head grew spikey, white hair; his nose lengthened; his muscles tightened; and he stretched a few inches taller. He groaned, leaning his forehead into the cradle of his arm.

When the shaking stopped, he glanced up with empty, honey-brown eyes. Bordock stepped out of the cubicle, then stretched his neck and shoulders, exhaling slowly as he did so.

This shapeshifting business was proving harder than anticipated, yet he knew he had no choice but to hold up the pretence that he was Connelly if he was to find Mesmo and the boy. Time was not on his side. He should have been gone long ago. Yet all trails of the fugitives had gone up in smoke. His pulse elevated at the mere thought.

His eyes fell on six, large circles outlined on the back wall of the ship—three above at eye-level and three directly below. Small lights blinked at him, inviting him over. He couldn't resist the temptation and pressed a couple of buttons on the lowest circle to the right. Immediately, a long tube ejected from the wall. It contained a form inside.

Bordock stared at the pale face with white lips and closed, sunken eyes of the man who lay in the tube before him. He noticed how a soft blue light reflected on the man's bald head.

"Enjoying the ride, Connelly?" Bordock smirked.

He noted with satisfaction that the features of the real Connelly were well preserved in the tube, meaning he would still be able to shapeshift into the agent. In fact, the man looked like he was sleeping peacefully. Bordock tapped on the small screen that should have indicated an extremely slow heartbeat brought on by induced sleep.

There was nothing.

"You'll have company soon enough," he promised the dead man.

Bordock let the real Connelly slide back into his unusual coffin, then tapped the other incubators for good measure. They would fit Mesmo and the boy, as well as Mesmo's other three companions, who lay on the last floor of the Dugout. Then, and only then, would he have the necessary proof that his task was complete and he could leave this repulsive planet behind.

With that in mind, he headed back to the front of the ship, where he called up an impressive amount of screens. He surveilled them with renewed determination. On one of these many screens, Mesmo's face appeared, while behind it an innumerable amount of live camera images flickered with thousands of faces on them: the computer scrambled to find a match.

Below it, the same operation was happening with Benjamin Archer's face.

As the night wore on, the alien shapeshifter searched

for the fugitives from within his spacecraft, while in the office a few feet away, he knew that Inspector Hao was doing precisely the same thing.

CHAPTER TWO

Poison

Wake up!

Some part of Benjamin Archer's mind was talking to him, but the words did not match the intense dream he was having. In it, he was caught in the middle of a lightning storm. He was surrounded by bright sparks that gave off bluish, electric charges which shot into the darkness, in such a way that he did not have time to figure out where he was. Were his feet even touching the ground? He didn't think so.

He became extremely apprehensive as the storm intensified. It reminded him of a girl with long, white hair. She was grasping his hand, staring at him fiercely as she discharged a flow of energy into his body.

He squirmed in his sleep, trying to escape

something he could not run from. But as he did so, he felt himself drop into darkness at an alarming speed. His arms flailed in a meek attempt to slow his fall, while a deep, repetitive sound reached his ears. Whatever it was, he was careening towards it.

Thud-thud, thud-thud it went, louder and louder.

A roaring sound reached his ears, and without warning, he was thrust into a thick liquid, surrounded by nasty, blue filaments.

Poison!

He writhed at the realization. The blue threads followed him into the dark-red rivers that were his own blood. His mind zoomed out and he saw the complex network of his veins, like a million tree-roots, heading in the same direction.

Thud-thud, thud-thud

In an instant, the blue poison would reach his heart and be pumped throughout his body.

He scrambled to stop this from happening, but it was as if he were swimming in dense water. His heart pounded like a drum, releasing the poison to every living cell, ingesting, expulsing, ingesting, expulsing.

Stop!

Wake up!

Two voices were fighting for attention, one internal, the other external.

How does that even make sense?

Wake up!

Ben's eyes fluttered open. He rolled to his side,

breathing heavily. He reached out to his bedlamp, but just as he flicked on the switch, he thought he saw a bluish halo around his hand. He blinked several times, now wide awake. He shut off the light again and stared at his hand; of course, it was normal. He leaned back into his pillow, switched on the light again, and took in the normalcy of his bedroom: a desk with a chair, a window with dark-blue curtains, a beige carpet, a bed with a thick, dark-brown duvet which he had half kicked off.

And Tike, who was staring at him with his tongue lolling from his place beside the nightstand. The white-and-brown terrier placed his paws on the side of the bed to lick his face.

Ben scratched the dog's ears absentmindedly. Was he ever going to have a normal nights' sleep again?

The blue filaments of his dream followed him as he got up, showered and dressed. A lump of fear grew in his throat, and he knew why: a second before waking, he had glimpsed the poison exiting his heart and spreading to the rest of his body.

It was too late, of course. The alien girl had infected him with the alien skill just over three months ago. Every cell of his body would have absorbed it by now.

Ben remembered Mesmo's words when he had asked him, "What if I don't want it?"

Mesmo had replied, "That question is irrelevant. It is part of you now. You should be happy."

Only, he wasn't.

Too much had happened for him to think about it

much, but as soon as Mesmo confirmed the alien element was part of him, a terrifying thought dawned on him.

I am no longer entirely human.

Ben knew, with unspoken certainty, that with every passing day, the infection was making him less and less human, and more and more alien.

Tike didn't seem affected by Ben's mood. He scampered down the stairs, then headed to the kitchen.

As Ben followed him, a man's voice reached his ears. He remembered that his mother had started a new job at a local Tim Horton's that morning, so the man was apparently talking on his cell phone. This was confirmed as soon as he entered the kitchen and found Thomas Nombeko sipping a cup of coffee with the phone stuck to his ear. The dark-skinned man thrust a couple of fingers in the air as a matter of greeting without letting go of the cup as he continued to speak.

Ben slipped into the chair of a small breakfast table and was about to reach for a slice of bread when he saw his mother's note. "Dear Ben, Enjoy your first day at school. Love, Mom."

He smiled, thanking his mother silently for her soothing words. They made him feel less alone. He grabbed the pen that she had used and wrote. "Thanks,

Mom. Enjoy your first day at work. Love, B." She had left at dawn, so he knew she would be back before him and would read the message on her return.

By the time he had spread peanut butter on his bread, Thomas had hung up and grinned at him. "Hey, kiddo! How did you sleep?"

"Fine, thanks," Ben answered automatically, reacting to the man's contagious smile, then remembering the dream. He swallowed the piece of bread through the lump in his throat.

Thomas sighed, a worried look passing briefly through his eyes. "That was work," he said, waving the cell phone at him. "They're asking me to fly a doctor to a town up north. Some kind of medical emergency." He put the phone away in his back pocket as he shook his head. "I promised your mom I'd take you in on your first day of school. You know, to show you around and all that. But now this came up..."

Ben studied his host's genuinely concerned face and said hurriedly, "It's ok. I can manage. I know what a school looks like." He tried to sound sincere, but an image of his old school and the two bullies, Peter and Mason, flickered through his mind.

He could tell that Thomas wasn't convinced. "I don't know. I promised your mom. Plus, we want to be able to face any awkward questions together." He bit his inner lip while he thought. "You could start tomorrow instead."

Ben considered this for a moment. Facing a whole class of new students did not sound particularly inviting, but spending a day alone with his thoughts was even less so. He breathed deeply to give himself courage.

Might as well get it over with.

"No, it's ok, really. You already took care of the administrative stuff, right?" When Thomas nodded, Ben continued, "So it's fine. I'm almost thirteen, you know? I'll find my way around. And if they ask anything, I'll tell them to contact you."

Thomas placed his empty cup in the dishwasher and beamed. "All right, kiddo. Gotta get those neurons working, eh?" He chuckled warmly as he headed out of the kitchen.

In the short week they had spent with the forty-three-year-old man, Ben had learned that their kind host was never one to worry for too long. He hoped the man's positive attitude would brush off on him. As a witness of The Cosmic Fall, who had had to give up his job as a postal worker in the town of Chilliwack and who had had to flee government intrusion by moving east to begin a new life, Ben considered that Thomas Nombeko had done quite well for himself.

After swooping Ben, Laura, Mesmo and Tike off Susan Pickering's island, Thomas had explained how he had been taking intensive flying lessons in Chilliwack before his life was turned upside down by the events that took place there. Yet, The Cosmic Fall had ultimately allowed him to fulfil his life-long dream of becoming a pilot. He had ended up in the small town of Canmore, on the edge of the Canadian Rocky Mountains in the

Province of Alberta, where the local Canmore Air Company was swift to hire him after he proved his flying skills. Ben laughed inwardly as he remembered the panicked look on Mesmo's face at the words "flying skills" while the hydroplane took them low along the West Coast to escape radar detection.

Thomas appeared in the kitchen doorway, covered in a thick, knee-length winter jacket, gloves and knitted hat. "Are you done with that yet?" he said, pulling Ben out of his thoughts and indicating his half-eaten piece of bread. "We have to get going."

Ben blinked, stuffing the rest in his mouth. "Wha'? A'ready?" He glanced at the clock on the wall. It was still early.

Thomas burst into laughter, showing his pearl-white teeth. "Have you looked outside yet, kiddo?"

Ben gulped down his milk and placed the cup in the dishwasher, glancing through the kitchen window as he did so. Everything was white.

"Oh!" he exclaimed, understanding Thomas' hurry.

"Yes, 'oh' is right." Thomas chuckled. "I'm going to need your help clearing the car out of the driveway. The sky dumped six inches of snow on us during the night. You'd better get used to it. They say we're headed into an unusually cold winter."

Ben opened the fridge door hurriedly. "Ok, give me a minute, I'll be right out." He'd forgotten he'd need to make his lunch. This going-back-to-school business was going to take some getting used to. He suddenly felt like he'd been thrown through a hurricane these past months and hadn't quite landed on his feet yet.

Inside the fridge were several small plastic containers with food in them and a post-it with a smiley face drawn on it. Ben felt a rush of warmth as he took out the neatly packed lunch.

"Thanks, Mom," he said to himself with a smile.

He placed everything in a backpack Thomas had lent him, then rushed to the front door before realizing he still had to put on his snow gear.

Sure, it snowed back west where he came from, but it only felt like yesterday since he had been spending his summer vacation at his grandfather's house. Now he was suddenly thrust into sub-zero temperatures and needed to think in terms of dark, gloomy days. He felt a pang of worry as he imagined himself sitting for hours in a new classroom while he tried not to think about everything that had happened to him, and everything that could still happen. He pushed the thought away and concentrated on pulling on his snow boots, warm jacket, scarf and gloves.

"C'mon, Tike," he said to the dog as he heaved his backpack on his shoulder. Leaving Tike behind did not even cross Ben's mind.

He opened the front door and was greeted with a street lined with townhouses, parked cars and snow-covered walkways. The snow removal trucks had already cleared most of the town, but Ben could tell that people were driving with care.

Thomas handed him a second snow shovel and

both set to work clearing the driveway in front of the car. When they settled in it, Thomas exclaimed, "Hang on a minute! I can't take Tike to work with me."

"He's coming with me," Ben interjected, to which Thomas raised an eyebrow. Ben glared at him to show him that that was the end of the discussion.

Thomas shrugged. "Fine by me," he said as he moved the car into the street. "Just remember it's a twenty-minute walk if they send you home. There's a bus, too. It's line twenty-five. You can take it when school lets out. The school said it's only three bus stops to my place." He pointed out some street names and landmarks so Ben could find his way back.

Finally, Thomas parked opposite the Lawrence Grassi Middle School. It was a large, low-lying building with an extensive, snow-covered playground around it. Children made their way to the main door, often stopping to throw a snowball at their friends.

"This is it," Thomas said in a low voice.

Ben figured he was scanning the surroundings to make sure everything was safe. He felt a small shiver run down his spine.

Thomas turned to him with genuine concern in his eyes. "Will you be ok?"

Ben nodded bravely. He picked up his backpack and got out of the car, managing a small "Thanks."

"Hey, kiddo," Thomas said urgently as Tike jumped out of the car after the boy. Ben bent his head to look at the man in the driver's seat. "What's your name?" Thomas asked.

Ben frowned at the question. "Benjamin Arch..." He began, then froze, his eyes going wide. He bent his knees, not so much to be at eye-level with Thomas, but rather because his legs had gone weak.

I almost fell for it!

"It's Ben Anderson," he said with a strained voice.

CHAPTER THREE

The Declaration

Ben gazed at Thomas, repeating to himself, "Ben Anderson, Ben Anderson..."

Thomas nodded tensely. "Ben Anderson. Not Benjamin Archer. This is important: it's the name I registered you under." He warned. "Don't forget."

Ben could tell Thomas was hesitating to let him go, so he nodded, stood back and closed the car door swiftly.

If I don't do this today, I'll never do it.

He crossed the road with Tike at his heels, feeling Thomas' gaze follow his every footstep. The lump in his throat magnified. How could he forget the story they had made up to cover their tracks and integrate into the town of Canmore?

He played the conversation he had had with Laura,

Mesmo and Thomas over in his mind so he wouldn't forget any details.

Thomas had suggested that Mesmo–whom they would call Jack Anderson–was his former colleague from back west. He had been laid off, so Thomas had offered him a job at Canmore Air. When Jack had accepted, he had brought his wife and son–Laura and Ben Anderson–to Canmore. Thomas was offering them a place to stay in his three-bedroom townhouse until the family could get back on their feet and find their own place to rent.

Ben thought it was a brilliant plan. He couldn't understand why his mother had gone crimson as she stuttered to find an alternative story. Did it bother her that much to pretend to be married to the alien?

When Ben suggested Laura wear the ring his real father had given her before he was born, Thomas broke into a wide grin. "Excellent! That's it, then. It's settled Mr. and Mrs. Anderson."

It had seemed pretty straightforward at the time, yet now that he was faced with reality, things suddenly felt a lot more complicated. He would have to watch every word that came out of his mouth. He had no choice. He knew that, although his mother wouldn't admit it, they had run out of money. The secret services had frozen her accounts so all they had was whatever bills and coins they had on them. They would have to lay low until they could figure out the next step. With that in mind, Ben entered his new school and headed to the administration, though not before looking for a secluded spot behind the school where he settled Tike with a warm blanket and crackers.

The curly-haired school receptionist peered at him as Ben said dutifully, "Hi, I'm a new student. My name is Ben Anderson. I'm in grade seven."

The woman broke into a smile. "Oh, welcome, Ben! We've been expecting you." She glanced around behind him as if searching for something. "Did you come on your own?"

Ben cleared his throat. "Yes, my mom had to go to work."

A look of sympathy crossed her face, though it was swiftly replaced by her smile. "Good on you, then, for taking the first step on your own. Now, let's see, you'll be in Ms. Amily Evans' class. That's in room 103. Let me get the Principal. She will want to take you there herself."

Ben opened his mouth to protest, but she disappeared into a side corridor, leaving him to wonder for the hundredth time whether he was ready for this.

The school bell rang and a throng of noisy students filled the entrance behind him.

The receptionist appeared several minutes later, followed by a petite woman with black, shoulder-length hair.

"This is Ben Anderson," the receptionist said, waving a hand at him. "He's the new student for Ms. Evans' class that Thomas helped register last week." She turned to Ben and said, "Ben, this is Mrs. Linda Nguyen, our school Principal."

The Principal smiled, studying him with small,

black eyes behind modern, black-rimmed glasses. "Hello, Ben. Welcome to Lawrence Grassi Middle School. I was looking forward to meeting you. Thomas says you're a bright student." She shook his hand firmly, gazing at him with sincerity. Ben immediately felt bad about having lied about who he really was.

"Come on, I'll take you to your class. You'll be impatient to meet your new friends." She led him down corridors covered in lockers which were stacked with winter clothes, chatting amiably about the amenities and after-school activities he could join. He was relieved that she didn't ask him any questions about his background. He knew that Thomas had covered the details when he had registered Ben.

A handful of late students hurried to their classrooms, greeting the Principal awkwardly as they passed. Mrs. Nguyen stopped in front of room 103. Once Ben had removed his winter clothes, she knocked before entering.

Ben's heart did a double flip as she ushered him inside. Twenty-four pair of eyes turned to look at him. He fully expected to be greeted by cold stares and sneering whispers.

"Good morning, class," Mrs. Nguyen said. "This is Ben Anderson. He'll be joining you as of today. I trust you will make him feel at home." It wasn't a question, but a statement. She nodded towards the teacher. "I'll leave you to it, Amily." She patted Ben lightly on the shoulder, before closing the door behind her.

Ben's teacher stood up from her desk and headed towards him. She had very short, brown hair and a youthful face. Her slim neck stuck out of a turtleneck sweater of a gray-blue colour. Ben liked her as soon as her mouth widened into a smile.

"Hi, Ben," she said. "I'm Ms. Amily Evans, your seventh-grade teacher. We're glad to see a new face around here, aren't we class?"

A wave of giggles reached Ben, though he found they weren't of a mocking kind. Some hands waved at him, and he heard a couple of *Hi, Ben*s.

"Let's find you a seat." Ms. Evans said, searching the room. Multiple hands shot in the air as several students shouted, "Over here!" One chubby boy in particular waved his hand wildly above his head. There was a free seat next to him by the window, on the opposite side of the classroom.

Ms. Evans placed a soft hand with long fingers on Ben's shoulder, where the Principal had patted him reassuringly moments ago as if it was some kind of unspoken gesture of comfort used by the school personnel. "Hm, yes," she said. "How about you sit next to Max, by the window?"

Ben nodded. He didn't trust using his voice yet. He made his way to his new spot, noticing the wide eyes and shy smiles from the other students on the way.

They're as nervous as I am!

It was a surprising thought, and he felt a weight lift partially from his shoulders.

They mustn't get many new students around here...

The realization struck him. He slid into his seat, feeling more relaxed by the minute. The bullying virus clearly hadn't affected this classroom because he didn't hear any jeering comments directed at him.

"So, Ben, where are you joining us from?" Ms. Evans asked.

Ben tensed in his seat.

Here we go with the questions.

"Hum, Vancouver."

"Ah!" Ms. Evans exclaimed knowingly. "I bet it's not as snowy as it is here yet!"

Ben shook his head, smiling. It would be several weeks–even months–before snow reached the West Coast.

Ms. Evans addressed the class. "It's not easy changing schools in the middle of the year so I expect everyone to lend a hand if Ben needs it. Let's show him some Canmore hospitality, all right?"

There were many nods of agreement.

"Ben, we have to get on with the class. Follow as best you can and come and see me during the first break please," Ms. Evans instructed.

Ben nodded, exhaling silently.

This isn't too bad, after all.

✳ ✳ ✳

By the time the last hour of class began, Ben felt as though the day had gone by in a blur. A considerable amount of information had been dumped on him, though everyone–teachers and students alike–had reassured him that he could ask questions or come to them for help anytime.

At lunch in the bright, roomy cafeteria, most of his classmates had hovered around him and fought about who would sit next to him. They had bombarded him with questions about his previous school and why he had moved to such a small town in the middle of the school year. Ben had fed them the story he had practiced with Thomas and Laura, though fortunately, they interrupted him so often that he hadn't gotten much of a chance to answer everything properly–which suited him fine.

Now, as he stared at the snowy landscape from his classroom window, he realized it had been strangely comforting to refer to Mesmo as his dad. He had never had the opportunity to call anyone dad before since his own father had passed away in a car crash after his birth. Referring to someone as dad stirred unknown feelings in him, even if the whole story was just pretence.

He blinked as he realized the teacher was already talking.

"...Declaration of Human Rights," Ms. Evans said, as she finished writing a website on the blackboard.

Ben straightened in his chair. It had been reassuring to find that he wasn't too far behind in most classes, which seemed to please his chubby neighbour greatly, as the boy regularly peeked at Ben's notes, whispering with wide eyes, "You've seen this already?" and "What did she say?" This material, however, was new to Ben, and he wondered where Ms. Evans was going with it.

She walked over to Ben's desk with a document in her hand as she spoke. "I'm sure you all consulted the United Nations' website, which I wrote on the blackboard, like I asked you to."

Many students scrambled to pull out the same-looking document from their backpacks.

Ms. Evans dropped the stapled pages on Ben's desk, saying quietly to him, "This is for civics class. Try and read up on it by next week, would you?"

Ben nodded and stared at the bold title on the first page: UNIVERSAL DECLARATION OF HUMAN RIGHTS. It was eight pages long and was printed off the UNITED NATIONS website. Ben scanned the pages curiously.

Ms. Evans leaned against the corner of her desk, locking her fingers before her. "So...who can refresh our memories and tell us what are the United Nations?"

A girl called Rachel shot her hand up in the air.

Ms. Evans waited for other hands to appear, but since none did, she pointed at the tall girl. Ben had already identified Rachel as the smart one in the class, yet was surprised to find she was not afraid to speak her mind. In his previous school, the bright students tended to avoid raising their hands, for fear of being reprimanded by less studious companions.

The dark-skinned girl answered with a clear voice, "It's an organization of countries that work together to bring peace to the world."

Ms. Evans smiled at her. "That's about right, Rachel. The United Nations is an international organization that promotes peace and co-operation throughout the world. Does anyone know where the headquarters are located?"

Someone shouted, "New York!"

"Right again," Ms. Evans said. "The United Nations was created in 1945, after the Second World War, to try and avoid such a terrible conflict from ever happening again. Now, what I wanted to talk about today is one of the most important documents that was signed at the United Nations by almost all the countries in the world." She waved the document at them.

"It is called the Universal Declaration of Human Rights. It contains thirty articles, which apply to all human beings. Since I'm sure you've all read the articles like I asked you to, maybe we could help Ben here by sharing some of them with him?"

Some students fidgeted nervously in their seats, while others glanced at the pages hurriedly. Rachel's hand shot in the air again.

"Yes, Rachel?"

"The thirty articles talk about how people's rights must be protected. Like the right to freedom or the right to life," Rachel explained proudly.

Ms. Evans agreed. "Yes. Each and every one of us has fundamental rights that must be protected at all costs.

We take for granted that we can go to school, go home to our families, travel freely to other countries or feel safe in the presence of the law. Yet you should not take these rights for granted. Many generations passed and many conflicts occurred before these rights were finally written down. Now, let's talk about these thirty articles. What types of rights do you think need protection?"

Some hands went in the air.

"The right to vote?" a girl called Kimberly said from the front row.

"Very good." Ms. Evans approved. "We all have the right to elect people that we would like to represent us in our government. Did you know that women weren't allowed to vote until the 1920's? And that there are still countries where women are not allowed to vote?"

"Children aren't allowed to vote!" a boy called Tyler noted. Everyone laughed.

"Hold on a second!" Ms. Evans smiled. "That is actually an excellent point, Tyler. Do you think children should be allowed to vote?"

"Sure!" He grinned. More laughter.

"Then why do you think they are not allowed to vote?" Ms. Evans asked.

Tyler shrugged.

Rachel had her hand up and answered before Ms. Evans had time to pick her. "Because you have to be eighteen to vote. You have to be a responsible adult."

Ms. Evans agreed. "That's right. This is an interesting topic which we will talk about later. But let's get back to our fundamental rights. What types of things do you take for granted, but would be afraid of losing?"

Only Rachel's hand was in the air. Most other students pouted at the document on their desk.

"My family?" someone ventured.

Ms. Evans agreed. "Yes, we all have the fundamental right to form a family and to live with our parents, brothers and sisters, husband or wife. No one may threaten our family. No one has the right to impose marriage on you, either. There must be mutual consent: both must agree to marry."

Ben saw Tyler make a vomiting gesture. His friend Wes sniggered beside him.

"What else?" Ms. Evans asked.

There were hesitant faces, so Ms. Evans said, "What about the right to life and freedom that Rachel mentioned earlier? Let's read Article 1 of the Declaration. 'All human beings are born free and equal in dignity and rights.' Or listen to this one. 'No-one shall be held a slave or tortured.' It took thousands of activists and hundreds of years to abolish slavery and protect freedom. The freedom to move around, to think freely, to choose your religion, to travel to another country without being afraid of imprisonment..." All eyes were fixated on their teacher.

"Here's another one related to freedom. 'No one shall be subjected to arbitrary arrest, detention or exile,' and, 'Everyone charged with a penal offence has the right to be presumed innocent until proved guilty.' I want you to think about this for a minute. Do you have any idea what this means?"

The students hung onto the teacher's every word.

"It means no one can be arrested and put into jail without proof of wrong-doing. The police need to find concrete proof that you did something very evil before they can arrest you. Unfortunately, there are countries where the opposite happens: first you are arrested and, while you are in jail, you must provide proof that you are innocent! In other words, you are presumed guilty until proved innocent! Can you imagine how scary that is? How can you defend yourself for something you didn't do, if you are already in prison?

"You see how important this document is? It protects all human beings from suffering unjustly. So let's see, what else should we be protected from?" She paused, but since no one spoke, she added, "What would you like to be protected from? What makes you afraid?"

Some students started chatting.

"War," one of them said.

"Losing my house."

"Starvation."

"Not being allowed to go to school." That was Rachel, of course.

"Monsters under my bed," Wes muttered.

Everyone burst out laughing.

"I hate spiders," Kimberly, who was playing with her long ponytail and munching on a piece of chewing-gum, told her two friends. Her comment carried over the laughter, triggering more guffaws and babbling, and suddenly the tenseness in the classroom evaporated.

Ben glanced at the teacher, thinking she would be upset at having lost the students' attention. Instead, Ms. Evans watched with a small smile as conversation erupted through the room. Kimberly, Alice and Joelle were three tight-knit girlfriends who Ben took to be the reasonably well-behaved lot. They spent most of their time chatting about their impeccable braids and ponytails, trendy clothing and lightly visible make-up. He had already gathered that they were not usually amused by the two boys, Wes and Tyler's, comments, which they apparently thought were childish and annoying.

Ms. Evans clapped her hands. "Ok, kids! It sounds like we're going to have to create a new Declaration. The Lawrence Grassi Declaration of Human Rights." She wrote on the blackboard. ARTICLE 31. NO ONE SHALL BE SUBJECTED TO THE FEAR OF LIVING WITH A MONSTER UNDER THEIR BED.

Giggles.

Ms. Evans turned around. "So, who's next?"

Ben grinned. Max had told him over lunch that Ms. Evans was the favourite teacher in the school. He understood why and admired her ability to veer the babbling back to the subject at hand.

"No one shall be subjected to the fear of snakes," someone said.

"Very good." Ms. Evans smiled.

Ben's neighbour ventured, "No one shall be subjected to thunder and lightning."

"Everyone has the right to sleep in on Sundays," Tyler shouted gleefully, triggering hoots of laughter.

A voice broke through the noise. "No one shall be subject to the fear of abandonment."

The laughter died down, and everyone turned to see who had spoken.

Ben spotted a girl wearing black clothes and a black beanie hat sitting, motionless, with her arms crossed before her. Her eyes were hidden behind black bangs that reached down to her chin in such a way that it was hard to tell what she actually looked like. He hadn't noticed her before.

"Kimi? Were you sharing your article with us?" Ms. Evans asked.

A silence fell over the classroom.

The girl repeated, "No one shall be subject to the fear of abandonment."

Wes snorted at the heaviness of the comment.

Ms. Evans ignored the rude reaction. "That's pretty deep, Kimi," she spoke to the girl. "We often think fear comes from live or inert things around us-like spiders or lightning-but in fact, the worst and strongest fears come from immaterial things, including from our own minds. You'll notice that most of the articles of the Declaration are immaterial, such as freedom and life. Good one, Kimi."

Ben continued to stare curiously at the girl.

"What about you, Ben? Would you like to share an article for our Lawrence Grassi Declaration with us? What would you like to be protected from? What is your worst fear?"

Ben's heart dropped like a stone. He turned around slowly to face the front of the classroom, fully aware that he had suddenly become the center of attention. A million thoughts flashed before his eyes.

Burning objects falling from the sky. Twisted Eyes. Poison coursing through his blood...

"Uh..." was all he could utter. He sweated profusely.

A handful of seconds passed, yet they felt like an eternity. Mocking smiles were creeping onto some faces.

Come up with something, you idiot!

"No one shall be subject to panic attacks," he blurted.

Scattered laughter.

He kept his hands under his desk to avoid anyone seeing them tremble.

"All right," Ms. Evans smiled acceptingly. "Speaking in front of a room full of unknown faces would trigger a bit of panic, I'd say! It sounds like you know what you're talking about!"

Some of Ben's tension ebbed away. Mentioning panic attacks had been the appropriate comment. His teacher obviously believed he was feeling shy about speaking in front of the class.

"Yeah, I used to have panic attacks," he admitted, glad to have found a safe subject and thinking she'd move on to the next student.

Instead, she said, "Really?"

Ben wrung his hands together under the table.

"You said *used to*. Does that mean you don't get them anymore?" she asked with genuine interest. She must have noticed his discomfort, because she added, "I'm sorry. I don't even know how we came to this theme. We're way off subject! Sneaky kids!" She wagged an accusing, yet playful finger at the class. "It just struck me that you named a fear that you don't seem to suffer from anymore. I was hoping you'd share how you did that with us...if you feel up to it, that is?"

Ben swallowed.

He realized he had expected most people to show indifference to his presence. Instead, it was the complete opposite in this classroom.

And then there was the panic attack thing. Ben hadn't really given it any thought, but the truth was that he hadn't had one in a long while. Had he really gotten rid of them?

Everyone waited for him to answer, so he cleared his throat. "Actually, I think it's thanks to Mes...hum...my dad. When he's around, I feel safe. I guess he's helped me put things into perspective."

Ben listened to his own words in amazement. Did Mesmo really have that effect on him? He had to admit, he always felt safer when the alien was around. Mesmo made his fears seem less overwhelming.

"Thank you for sharing, Ben," Ms. Evans smiled encouragingly. "Putting things into perspective is an excellent way to face your fears. I mean, seriously, how many of us are scared of spiders?"

Several hands went up in the air, including Ms. Evans'.

"Now think how big you are compared to a tiny spider," she continued. "You could step on it without a second thought. It should be more afraid of you than you are of it! You see, when you truly understand the thing that you fear, you'll be able to put it into perspective, and you'll realize that maybe your fear is unfounded."

Ben tried to picture Bordock as a tiny spider. It didn't work.

Ms. Evans rubbed her hands together. "Anyway, let's get back to our Declaration. We're talking about much bigger things than spiders. We're talking about protecting the whole of humanity against serious threats such as war, loss of life, loss of freedom, slavery, etc. Pretty fearsome things, I would say." She picked up a copy of the Declaration. "Let's read article twenty-six."

Ben sagged back into his chair, his mind buzzing.

CHAPTER FOUR

Kimimela

Not long after, the school bell rang. Ben jumped as several chairs screeched back, releasing students from their desks. He realized almost everyone had been paying close attention to the time and had slowly been feeding their backpacks so that, as soon as the bell chimed, they were ready to dart out of class.

Pull yourself together!

His first day back at school had been more of a roller-coaster ride than he had expected.

"Are you taking the bus?" Max asked.

Ben looked up in surprise. "Huh? Oh, yes. I'm taking the twenty-five."

Max heaved his backpack over his shoulder. "Yeah,

most of us are. I can show you where it is."

Tike.

"Oh, hum, that's ok. I need to sort out a couple of things before I leave."

"Oh, 'kay. See you, then," Max said, sounding disappointed.

"I'll catch up with you," Ben offered.

Max's face brightened. "'kay." He waved shyly and headed out.

By the time Ben left the classroom, most of his companions had gone. He grumbled inwardly when he remembered he had to put on all his winter gear again. While he struggled with his boots, he saw Kimi leaning her right foot against a low shoe-cabinet, tying the laces of army boots. Observing her curiously out of the corner of his eye, he noticed that everything about her was black: boots, jeans, a knee-length jacket, long side bangs and beany hat.

What a gloomy girl.

He cleared his throat. "That was a pretty deep thing you said–you know–about fearing abandonment?" he ventured.

Her head shot up, and her black eyes pierced him accusingly. "Yeah! Look who's talking. The boy with the super dad. Aren't you lucky?" she snapped.

Before he could react, she placed her heavy boot on the floor and stomped off.

Ben stared at her with his mouth open.

What's up with her?

He shook his head in disbelief. At least that reaction was closer to what he had been expecting all day, so it didn't bother him too much. He wrapped his scarf around his neck, then followed the girl from a safe distance. He slipped to the side of the school where he had left Tike. His dog peeked at him from behind a wall, then rushed out to greet him. Ben knelt to rub his back.

"Hey there! What's that?" A voice burst out from behind him.

Ben whirled around to find a man in a basic coverall staring at him.

"Is that your dog?" the man asked.

Ben swallowed. It was no use denying it. "Yes," he said, looking at the ground. To his surprise, the man bent to scratch Tike behind the ears.

"Hi, you! What's your name?" he said in a friendly voice. The dog grinned.

"His name is Tike," Ben offered.

"You're a good dog, aren't you?" the man said to the terrier.

Ben watched curiously.

The man stood, then offered his hand.

"I'm Joe, the school caretaker," he said.

"Ben Anderson," Ben answered, shaking the man's hand. "I'm new," he added as an afterthought as if that excused his dog being there.

"Well, Ben Anderson, I take it you know animals aren't allowed on the school grounds?"

Ben looked at his feet. He couldn't picture a day

without Tike nearby.

Joe pursed his lips. "Come, I think I may have a solution." He gestured for Ben to follow him until they reached a utility door with a sign that read FURNACE ROOM. Joe opened it to reveal humming machines inside. A whiff of warm air escaped the room. "This isn't exactly ideal, but you could leave Tike here while you're in class. I can check up on him and give him a couple of breaks outside during the day. I don't mind. I have dogs of my own. And you can pick him up here. Just make sure you don't forget him, 'cause I lock up the school at 6 pm."

Ben grinned, unable to believe his luck. "Thanks!" he said earnestly.

This is perfect!

"That's it, then. Off you go. If you hurry, you might catch the bus." Joe ushered him out.

Ben waved, then he and Tike sprinted across the playground. He could see busses filling up with school children. Max's red backpack stood out in the crowd. Ben headed in the same direction and made it just as the last students settled into their seats.

The back of the bus was rowdy. Tyler and Wes occupied the back seats, talking loudly. Max sat a few rows forward. The curly-haired boy waved and slid over into the empty seat by the window.

"I saved you a spot," Max said, fishing a big bag of cookies from the open backpack on his lap.

"Thanks!" Ben spoke out of breath as the bus departed. Tike jumped onto his lap.

"Whoa!" Max exclaimed, hugging his cookies.

Ben laughed. "Don't worry. Tike won't eat them." He scratched Tike's ears, noticing the forlorn look the dog was giving him.

Max shrugged and dug into the bag. "Wan' one?" he asked Ben while he stuffed his mouth.

Ben helped himself to a cookie and made sure some crumbs fell onto his lap as he bit into it. Tike was quick to notice. As he chatted with Max, Ben spotted a person dressed in black on the sidewalk. A blast of cold air hit him in the neck.

"Hey, Kimimela!" Tyler shouted out the back window. "My monsters won't abandon you. You want them?"

Ben whirled and caught Kimi making an obscene gesture at Tyler. Wes cried with laughter.

"Shut up, Tyler!" Ben yelled. The words were out of his mouth before he realized it.

Tyler pulled his head away from the window, startled. His face flushed, but not with anger. He shrugged sheepishly and closed the window, then flopped down next to Wes, eyeing Ben with a touch of respect. The noise in the bus died down a bit.

Ben settled into his seat again, his arms crossed across his chest. Hearing one kid making fun of another made his blood boil. It wasn't the girl's fault if she was an outsider. He, for one, knew exactly how that felt.

Max hadn't budged; he was still chomping away. He offered Ben the cookie bag. "Don't mind her," he said.

"She wants to be alone."

Ben considered this as he took a bite. "What did Tyler call her? I thought her name was Kimi?"

"Kimimela," Max corrected.

"Kimimela? That's a strange name. I've never heard it before."

Max stuffed a cookie in his mouth. "Dats cuz' it's naydiv."

Ben stopped munching. "Naydiv?"

Max swallowed hard. "No, dummy. *Native*, like, Native American. You know...?"

Ben stopped bringing the cookie to his mouth, his eyes widening in understanding. "Oh, I see. She's First Nation, then."

"Only half," Max explained. "Her mom's from the Dakhona Reservation. I don't think she lives there anymore, though." A boy sitting behind them tapped Max on the shoulder and asked for a cookie. Max turned to chat with him.

Ben stared out the window, lost in thought. He recognized a shop window and suddenly remembered he lived only three bus stops away from the school.

"I gotta go!" he said, picking up his backpack hurriedly. Tike slipped to the ground and caught the last of his cookie. "Bye." He waved at Max.

The back of the bus erupted, "Bye, Ben!"

Ben grinned at Wes and Tyler as they shouted their goodbyes gleefully.

"See you tomorrow!" Wes yelled in a sing-song

voice, waving his arm in the air like a ballerina. Just before reaching the door, Ben saw Tyler shove his friend into the window, so Wes' arm hung limp above his head. "Aargh!" the boy groaned with heavy exaggeration.

Ben shook his head. Those two clowns were rowdy but harmless.

He hopped down the steps, almost walking straight into Mesmo as he landed on the snowy walkway. He straightened to take in the tall alien standing before him.

The doors slid closed and the bus took off in a roar.

"Hi," Ben said through the sound of the motor.

"Hi," Mesmo replied.

Ben ignored Wes and Tyler as they sped by with their faces plastered against the bus window, their mouths open in crazy grins and their noses flattened against the windowpane.

"New friends?" Mesmo asked.

Ben snorted. "Not really," he said, then shrugged. "Maybe."

Facing Mesmo always stirred inscrutable feelings deep inside of him. Chatting about simple things such as a school day seemed trivial when faced with a being from a distant planet who had crossed the universe in a spaceship that far surpassed any human technology. It always took Ben a couple of giddy seconds to accept this information before he felt comfortable enough to speak with the alien.

"Should you be here?" he asked finally.

Mesmo checked his surroundings, frowning. "Do I look out of place?"

Ben considered the alien man who was wearing jeans, a brown jacket and a curious fur hat with ear flaps. Aside from his height and one strand of white hair peeking out from under the hat, he fit quite well among humans.

"It'll do," Ben said. "At least your hat is appropriate for this climate." He indicated the snowy city street. The few pedestrians wore different types of hats to fend off the cold. "I'm more worried that someone might step into you." He reached out and passed his hand through Mesmo's arm. He found it fascinating to observe the fabric of Mesmo's clothes, the details of his hands, the tiny hairs of his fur hat. Everything looked completely solid. Yet—he knew—the man who apparently stood before him was not really there. Not physically anyway.

"I don't remember calling you," Ben pondered, checking that his silver wristwatch with the spirit portal was safely attached to his arm.

Mesmo gave him a small smile. "You don't need to. Our bond is growing stronger. The portal is now always open to me. I can come and go as I please."

Ben stared at the snow wondering whether he liked that piece of information or not.

"Let's go," he said, subdued.

They walked side by side towards Thomas' house.

Footprints.

The word formed in Ben's mind, making him glance back.

Tike stared at him, then sniffed at the snow.

"Oh!" Ben exclaimed. "You're not leaving any footprints!" Both he and Mesmo observed the ground behind them. There was only one set of footprints in the snow and they belonged to Ben. He stared at the alien quizzically.

Mesmo smiled. "Well now, that is something I can remedy." A soft glow appeared around his hands, and as he put one foot in front of the other, the snow under his feet melted.

Ben watched the patches of walkway appearing next to his own footprints.

Of course! Mesmo can manipulate water, and snow IS water!

He grinned and nodded approvingly. "Cool!"

CHAPTER FIVE

The Crow

The weeks would have gone by smoothly if it hadn't been for what happened on a Tuesday morning.

Ben got used to catching up on homework, helping Max understand assignments and the three girlfriends—Alice, Joelle and Kimberly—making annoyed comments when Tyler and Wes cracked rude jokes in class. The gloomy girl, Kimi, brooded at the back of the class and avoided contact with anyone. But all in all, Ben was quite content going about his normal school activities with his friendly classmates.

The problem, however, didn't come from school. It came from an entirely unexpected source. And that source was Tike.

Never in a million years would Ben have thought

that he'd have any kind of issue with his four-legged friend, but that Tuesday morning, something that he had refused to accept so far was thrust into the light.

He was running late and hurriedly finished lacing his snow boots to his feet.

Drats! I forgot my gloves upstairs!

He considered untying the boots again so he wouldn't dirty the carpet but then decided against it. He'd have to do without gloves that day. He zipped his jacket, thrust his backpack on his shoulder and shoved the key into the front door to lock it.

"Tike!" he called, realizing the dog was still inside.

His terrier zipped through the door to join him outside and wagged his tail enthusiastically. Ben's gloves were clamped in his mouth.

Ben stiffened. Had he spoken aloud when he remembered his gloves? He was pretty sure he hadn't. He reached out to take the gloves from Tike's mouth, but froze again. A blue halo of light surrounded his hand. He jumped back, staring at it in fright.

He heard the blood rushing to his ears, and his heart began to thump harder.

Thud-thud, thud-thud.

He shut his eyes tight and shook his head—as if that would rid him of a reality he refused to accept.

He already knew that Tike was trying to use the alien skill to communicate with him. He had suspected it for quite some time, but no matter how wonderful the idea seemed, he would not, could not, accept it, for accepting it meant opening up to the alien poison in his blood. It meant accepting that he was becoming an anomaly, a mutated being that was neither human nor alien. Hadn't Inspector Hao glimpsed Ben's true self when he had said, "I know what you are!"

Not *who*. But *what*.

He was turning into a *thing*.

"Hey, kiddo! Time to go!" Thomas called from the driveway.

Ben held his glowing hands close to his body, nodding vaguely in Thomas' direction. He noticed that Tike was no longer wagging his tail, but stared at him curiously. Ben found he could not stare back at his own dog. He concentrated on putting on his gloves, his brain fighting to shut Tike out, and in so doing, shut out the skill.

I have to ignore it.

That was his only remedy. If he ignored the skill's existence, there was a chance it would weaken. Maybe it would even disappear altogether. The problem with that strategy was this: he would have to ignore Tike as well.

Ben didn't think about it further until he picked up Tike after school. The sight of his dog brought the incident back to his mind and he found himself reluctant to look at Tike's eyes. Instead, he said, "C'mon, let's hurry, or we'll miss the bus."

They left the school from the side door, but instead of heading for the bus stop, Tike suddenly darted away from Ben in the opposite direction.

"Tike!" Ben yelled. The terrier was already halfway across the football field, heading toward a row of trees.

"Tike! Come here!" Ben called again, annoyance creeping into his voice. He jogged after the dog, then slowed down when he realized a form was crouching in front of some bushes.

Ben frowned. "Tike?" he said more slowly.

The person's head turned to face the dog, and Ben recognized the long side bangs as they slipped before the girl's eyes. Kimi shoved the strand of hair behind her ear and made a gesture as if to block Tike from moving forward.

When she noticed Ben approaching, she threw him an angry glare. "Hey! Is that your dog?" she shouted. "Call him off!"

Ben reached her side. "It's ok. He's friendly," he said reassuringly.

No need to overreact.

But she was no longer looking at him. Instead, Ben realized both the girl and his dog had spotted something low in the bushes. Branches rustled, revealing a black crow that cawed loudly, thrashing around wildly as it tried to free itself.

Ben's gloved hands warmed abnormally. Blood rushed to his ears, accompanied by a wave of intense fear. Stars swam before his eyes, and he almost retched as an overwhelming pain made his left arm go limp. He dropped to his knees in the snow, wincing.

Kimi, who was carefully pushing aside some

branches, must have thought he had gasped in surprise, because she said, "Sh! Don't make a noise. I think it's hurt. And pull your dog away. He's scaring it."

Ben blinked tears from his eyes and tried to ignore the staggering pain that drowned his thoughts. He inhaled silently several times, almost drowning in the bird's fear as it coarsed through his brain.

Don't be afraid.

He directed the thought at the crow, trying to counter the bird's panic. It eyed him with beady, black eyes, its wings spread at a strange angle, its beak half open. From a corner of his brain, Ben observed his huge self from the bird's eyes. His heart raced in combined rhythm with the crow's. The fear that grasped his mind was not his, yet he felt it to the core. He vaguely registered Kimi speaking next to him and tried to concentrate on what she was saying, though her words sounded foreign.

"I think its wing is broken," Kimi said. "I've tried to catch it, but it keeps flapping around and getting stuck further in."

It hurts!

Ben's head exploded with words that were not his. And searing pain throbbed through his own arm. His heart raced, *thud-thud, thud-thud* and for a second he lost himself completely in the crow's mind. Frantically, he sent soothing thoughts to the bird.

I'll help you.

The crow gave up flapping and regarded him with the eyes of a trapped animal. They stared at each other, each assessing plausible dangers. The fear in Ben's mind subsided somewhat and he was able to think more clearly.

Don't be afraid.

He sent the thought to the crow again, more clearly this time, and it bowed its head in acceptance. Ben reached out to it.

"No!" Kimi pushed his arm away. "It'll peck at you!"

He heard her as if from somewhere far away. Removing his scarf, he held it from both ends and slowly approached the crow.

It's ok. Trust me.

He wrapped his hands carefully around the tense body, ignoring the searing pain in his arm. With the greatest care not to touch its broken wing, Ben lifted the bird and wrapped it in his scarf. By the time he stood again, his mind had cleared somewhat, and he realized that Kimi was staring at him with her mouth open.

"Wow!" she breathed. "How did you do that?"

Ben hoped his inner struggle wasn't showing on his face. He shrugged and replied, "I have a way with animals, I guess."

Kimi snorted, "Yeah, I'll say!" She frowned, considering him with worried eyes. "Are you ok? You look like you saw a ghost."

No, I'm not ok.

Cold sweat accumulated on his forehead. He felt sick, like his stomach was in his throat; his legs were weak. "I should take it to a vet," he said unsteadily. "Do you know any?"

An indefinite emotion flickered over the girl's eyes, but Ben couldn't tell what it was because her long strand of black hair hid half her face.

"Yes, I know one," she replied without much enthusiasm. She picked up her backpack and added, "Come on." She headed off with Ben following.

He found himself on the very sidewalk where Tyler had shouted at Kimi from the bus several days back.

As if reading his mind, Kimi slowed down, so they were walking side by side. "I heard about what you said to Tyler on the bus the other day," she said. "You didn't have to do that."

Ben gave her a sideways smile. "Tyler's a jerk."

To his surprise, her laugh came out crystal clear and authentic. He liked it immediately. "Wes, too!" She agreed, grinning.

They chatted sporadically, Ben having to stop to catch his breath once in a while and to shift the bird's weight away from his aching arm.

Twenty minutes later, Kimi led him away from the street and into a back alley. They passed snow-covered yards and garden sheds until they reached a property with a brick structure that was detached from the main house. Kimi opened a low fence and let him through. Then she fished some keys from her jacket pocket, one of which she inserted in the door lock of the small building. When Ben glanced inside the dim room, he found a curious table in its center while cabinets lined the back wall. A couple of animal cages were stacked against the side.

Kimi switched on a bright, neon light, then hurried across the room to grab one of the cages, which she placed on the table.

"Here," she said. "You can put the crow in the cage for now."

Ben did so reluctantly, ignoring its caws. "So...uh...where are we exactly?" he asked.

She avoided his eyes. "I live here," she said, pointing vaguely at the house opposite the square building. When Ben continued to stare at her quizzically, she sighed and added, "My mom's a vet. She doesn't practice anymore, though. She's been...sick."

"Oh," Ben said, studying the room again. Suddenly the central table, the cabinets containing medical supplies, and the animal cages made sense.

Kimi headed to the door. Still without looking at him, she said, "Wait here. I'll get my mom."

He watched her leave, a slight frown above his brow.

It's as if she didn't want me here.

Pain!

Ben whirled to face the crow in the cage. The blood rushed to his ears again and he could not control it. The crow stared at him with its tiny, round eyes, oblivious to the boy's inner struggle. A cold ripple travelled up and down Ben's back. So, was this going to be his new reality? Was he going to feel every animal's pain and thoughts? He wanted to cry from despair. He could barely stand the feelings of one creature. How was he ever going to survive the burden of thought from the whole animal kingdom?

And with each contact, he could sense the blue filaments in his blood multiplying, anchoring themselves into his very being. He still had his gloves on, but he could feel his hands warming with alien power. A wave of nausea washed over him and he had to hold on to the table for support.

The crow thrashed, causing searing pain to shoot up Ben's arm every time the bird hit the cage.

"Stop it!" Ben muttered through gritted teeth, before realizing he was no longer alone. He turned to find Kimi, followed by a woman.

The woman was slightly taller than him, had long, straight black hair to her waist, dark eyes, thin lips and elegant features. She must have been stunning at some point, but right now she was wearing an old sweater and she seemed very tired. Even with Kimi's beanie hat and side bangs, the resemblance to her mother was striking.

"This is my mom, Maggie," Kimi explained, sounding as though she was trying to excuse the woman's unkempt appearance. "Mom, this is Ben Anderson."

Maggie stared at Ben with intelligent eyes, then turned her attention to the crow. She pulled the bird out of the cage, then carefully unwrapped it from its makeshift nest in Ben's scarf. Speaking to Kimi in a language he couldn't understand, she examined it.

"It has a broken wing," she stated finally in English, confirming Ben's diagnosis. She gently stretched out the bird's wings one at a time, revealing beautiful, shiny feathers that reflected a bluish tint under the artificial light.

Ben bent in for a closer look. He had never seen a crow up close before. "She's beautiful!" he exclaimed.

Maggie glanced at him. "She?"

He distanced himself from the table. Had he really said that?

Maggie concentrated on the bird but addressed him. "You know your birds," she said. Ben bit his inner cheek nervously.

Maggie placed the crow back in its cage and busied herself in the medicine cabinets. "You say you brought this bird without getting a scratch?" she asked, eyeing Ben with piercing eyes.

Kimi stepped in, "Yes, *Iná*[1]. It's as if the crow knew we wanted to help it. It didn't struggle at all."

"Hm…" she said thoughtfully, before adding, "not many would save a crow. They are not popular animals. Yet they are particularly clever and have a great memory. They live in large groups called a 'murder of crows'." She paused, throwing Ben a glance. "But then, you probably knew that already."

"Ugh! Mom!" Kimi interjected, clearly irritated.

Ben sensed the strain in Kimi and Maggie's relationship. He tried to steer the conversation away. "Can you help her?" he asked, rubbing at his arm.

Maggie pulled out some medical supplies and said, "Yes, I will reset her wing and feed her so she will survive

---

[1] *Iná* = mother in 'Dakhona'.

the winter. We should be able to release her in a month." As she turned back to the table, she spotted Tike sitting by the door. "And who's this?" she asked.

"Oh, that's my dog, Tike," Ben answered. "He's a Jack Russell Terrier."

"Yes, I can see that. Six years old, I'd say. Though there's something unusual about him. He hasn't barked once at the bird..."

Kimi's eyes widened. "That's true! I've never heard him bark."

Ben shifted uncomfortably. This was not the way he wanted the conversation to go. He was extremely aware of the crow nearby, nagging at his mind. "Tike never barks," he said vaguely.

Maggie frowned and headed over to Tike. "I wonder why that is," she said, bending to scratch Tike's ears. "I could check him out..."

"No!" Ben interjected too quickly. Maggie glanced at him, frowning, so he added, "Thank you, but maybe some other time? Er...I actually have to go now. My mom will be wondering where I am."

I need air.

He nodded towards Kimi. "Sorry, I didn't realize how late it was. I'll see you tomorrow."

"Oh, ok," Kimi said, sounding disappointed.

Ben picked up his backpack a little too quickly, feeling their eyes burning into his back as he left. He hurried down the back alley and paused next to the side of a house. In his mind's eye, he was lying on the examination table. The woman with the black eyes stared at him. She applied a pressure on his arm that hurt so badly his eyes watered and he retched. He swore he could physically feel the alien venom spreading through his body. He shivered, though not because of the cold air. He was cold inside. Cold from fear.

"Ben?"

He jumped at Mesmo's voice. He held his jacket tightly around him, staring at the alien. "Jeez! You have to stop doing that!"

"Doing what?"

"Appearing out of nowhere like that. You startled me," Ben replied, catching his breath.

The man surveyed him, then frowned, "What's the matter? Are you sick?"

Turning away, Ben said, "It's nothing,"

Mesmo insisted. "Benjamin?"

"I told you! It's nothing!" Ben snapped. He strode off, his shoulders hunched, his hands deep in his pockets.

CHAPTER SIX

Enceladus

Laura heard the front door open and close. She stepped out of the kitchen, her hands laden with dinner plates, just in time to see Ben rush up the stairs to his room. Laura dropped the dishes on the table and joined Mesmo by the door.

"What's the matter?" she asked. Not waiting for a reply, she climbed the steps and saw Ben shut his bedroom door, almost hitting Tike on the nose. Tike jumped back, his ears laid back, one paw off the ground.

Laura knocked on the door. "Ben? Are you all right?" When there was no reply, she knocked again. "Ben?"

His muffled voice came through. "Long day, Mom. I just want to lie down for a while."

Laura bit her lip, hesitating, then picked up Tike in

her arms. Scratching his neck, she reassured him. "Don't worry, Tike. He'll get over it." She headed back down the stairs, adding, "Come on, let's go for a walk."

Tike hopped out of her arms, his tail wagging.

"Can I join you?" Mesmo asked.

Laura felt her cheeks flush, so she bent to put on her boots. "Yes, of course. Let's go out back. There's less chance we'll run into anyone."

Once she had on her winter gear, they headed out through the kitchen door, which led to a small, fenced yard, then open landscape for as far as the eye could see. She gazed at the snow-covered fields to the right, the low hill before them, and an impressive string of mountain ranges to the left. They were at the edge of the Canadian Rocky Mountains, which dramatically cut the skyline with their jagged peaks.

Tike scampered off in front, sticking his snout in snow mounds, no doubt searching for hidden rodents.

Laura glanced sideways at the alien, noticing his grayish skin. She felt a pang of worry. "Are you holding up?" she asked, drawing her eyebrows together.

He nodded but did not look at her.

"Tell me about today," she said. Laura knew he expected the question because she asked him the same one every day. He gazed into the distance, then answered mechanically, "Nothing new. Same, bare room: a hospital bed, a large mirror, cameras in the ceiling..."

"Any contact?" she pressed.

He shook his head. "They pushed the food tray

through the slit at the bottom of the door—same as always. Hamburger, fries, apple slices, orange juice... No contact."

"Hm," Laura said half to herself. "Until their boss returns..." She stared at the ground as she walked, deep in thought, going over the details in her mind. They had already determined that Mesmo was being held closer to the East coast, though in Canada or the US was not yet clear. They had figured this out because of the regular times Mesmo was being fed, which was twice a day. Only, they had calculated that the evening for Mesmo was early afternoon for Laura, meaning he was two or three hours ahead of her.

She glanced at the tall alien again, noticing that his cheekbones were more pronounced. *He's losing weight,* she thought, picturing a diet of soggy hamburgers. Something clicked in her mind—something that Ben had said before their departure to Canmore. "I'm turning vegetarian," her son had said. His comment had seemed to have nothing to do with Mesmo, but for some reason, it made Laura stiffen. "Are you eating?"

He turned his head away.

"Mesmo!" she gasped, her hand covering her mouth as she guessed the answer. "You don't eat meat, do you?" The realization sent a shiver down her back.

He still did not face her. "I have no appetite," he said finally. "The food on this planet is strange to me."

Laura stared at him with wide eyes, realizing where his unhealthy appearance came from.

"Mesmo!" she said worriedly, "You have to tell

them! You have to eat something! I'm serious! You have to keep up your strength to give us time to find you!"

"I am running out of time..." she heard him say.

"Don't give up!" Laura pleaded. "We'll get you out, I promise."

"That's not it," he said, turning to her at last. "I must complete my mission and reach Enceladus within four full Earth moons. After that, it will be too late."

Taken aback, Laura frowned. "What do you mean?"

"Every two hundred Earth years, the planets of your solar system align in such a way that their gravitational pull causes abnormal friction at a location near Enceladus. This opens a window between our galaxies, allowing us to travel from my home planet to Earth and back for a limited time. That window to my galaxy will close in four full moons or approximately one hundred and twenty Earth sunrises."

Laura sucked in a breath. She hadn't expected such a mind-boggling answer. Once again, she realized how little she knew about this man and where he came from. "You mean..." She swallowed. "...that if you don't make it to this Enceladus within four months, you'll be stuck here for two hundred years?"

His honey-coloured eyes fell on hers. "Yes," he replied.

Her heart dropped like a stone. "Mesmo," she said gently, not wanting to add more to his misery. "Aren't you forgetting something? Even if we free you from whoever is holding you, you don't have a spaceship."

He glanced sideways at her. "Bordock has a ship."

She fell silent, reeling from the task ahead. How were they ever going to free Mesmo, complete his mission—whatever it was—and find Bordock's ship in four months? She couldn't even begin to understand how long it would take him to reach this Enceladus, but anything located in outer space sounded impossibly far.

They headed back, walking in silence. She wished she could tell him something encouraging. About to push open the kitchen door, she had an idea. "What about the spirit portal? Couldn't you send your spirit to your planet? Send a message? Ask for help?"

She released the door and faced him. He stood close and she could see the details of his jacket and the fabric of his shirt. She caught herself longing to touch him. He smiled, and she noticed his teeth stood out pearl white in his olive-tanned skin. The walk in the open had done him good.

"Spirit portals have limited power. Their reach is only within your solar system. The signal would distort and dissipate within the contact point between our galaxies," he explained. "It may seem that my spirit is free to travel great distances, but the truth is it remains bound to the spirit portal. That is why I am always near Ben. I am caught in an invisible bubble of which the spirit portal—hence, Ben—is the center." He shook his head. "The spirit portal is not the answer."

"Fine," she said. "We'll find another way. But until then, you have to promise me something."

His brow lifted. "What?"

"Eat!" she ordered.

∗ ∗ ∗

Laura knocked on Ben's door again but did not wait for an answer. This time she stepped into his room, followed by Tike who jumped onto the boy's bed.

Ben's head was propped against his pillow with a document in his hand and surrounded by school books.

"Thomas brought Chinese food. Want to come down?" she asked.

Without looking up from his reading, he answered, "Sure, I'll be right there."

Laura hesitated, then went to sit at the edge of his bed. She sifted through the books. "Lots of homework?"

Ben sighed and sat up, dropping the document beside him. "No, it's ok. I can handle it."

She hoped he would open up more, but since he didn't add anything, she said, "I know it's hard, starting over. Especially in a new school with new friends. Just hang in there while I get us back on our feet again, ok?"

He shrugged. "Actually, it's not too bad. They've been pretty friendly so far."

Laura nodded. "Same here. I'm beginning to like this town."

"Me, too." Ben's brief smile disappeared.

"Is something the matter?" she asked, reading his face like it was her own. She touched his left arm, but he pulled it away and she thought she saw him wince.

"I'm fine."

She noticed he wouldn't meet her eyes.

"It's just," he hesitated, searching for words. "I'm not sure where I belong."

"I know," Laura said, staring at the floor. "I feel the same." Their eyes finally met. "It's normal to feel like that, at your age," she added. "But our situation obviously doesn't help." She patted his leg. "I promise I'll find us a place where we can belong."

His eyes lowered. "Look at me," she said. He did. "I promise you," she insisted. "Do you believe me?"

He nodded, but his eyes had drifted away again.

As she descended the stairs, Laura found Mesmo and Thomas bending towards each other, concentrated on a deep conversation. When they heard her approach, they distanced themselves, and the frown on Thomas' brow disappeared. He broke into a grin and he clapped his hands. "Come on, dinner is getting cold!"

CHAPTER SEVEN

Gift

A week later, Ben found Ms. Evans with a smug smile on her face. He glanced around at the rest of the students as he organized his pens and books on his table. Several of them were grinning.

Did I miss something?

He figured they had been telling a joke before he arrived, so he ignored them and sat at his desk.

"'Morning, class," Ms. Evans greeted them.

"'Morning, Ms. Evans," the students chanted back.

Still smiling, Ms. Evans glanced in Ben's direction. "I don't think Ben knows our tradition yet. So how about we put some extra effort into it?"

Ben stared around the classroom in bewilderment.

What's going on?

"Ready? One, two, three! Happy birthday to you, happy birthday to you..."

They all chanted extra loudly, while Ben's face flushed in surprise.

When they finished singing, Ms. Evans handed a card to him, saying warmly, "Happy thirteenth birthday, Ben. Everyone signed a card for you. We always sing when it's someone's birthday so you'll be hearing this a lot this year."

Ben grinned as he accepted the card. He turned around to survey the back of the classroom, but Kimi wasn't there. She had been absent ever since the crow incident. He whispered to Max, "Is Kimi sick?"

The round-cheeked boy shrugged. "'Dunno." He glanced at Ben's backpack hopefully. "Did you bring cupcakes?"

Later, after school, Ben came home to a delicious smelling house.

His mom stepped out of the kitchen with a broad smile. "Happy birthday, Ben!" she said, hugging him. "Did you have a good day?"

He showed her the birthday card. He had never gotten this much attention from his classmates before, so this day had turned out to be quite special. He started telling her about it, but loud grumbling burst from the kitchen.

"Are you all right in there, Thomas?" Laura yelled from the living room.

Thomas appeared in the doorway. "Darn onions!"

he said, wiping his eyes with a kitchen towel. Then he spotted Ben and his face brightened. "Hey, kiddo! Happy birthday!" He squeezed Ben, then lifted him up.

Ben squirmed. "Put me down!" he protested, laughing.

Thomas put him back on his feet and pretended to have a fist-fight with him. Ben copied him, dancing from one foot to the other, launching fake punches at the man, then ended up on the couch with Thomas tickling him in the ribs. Tike ran from one to the other excitedly.

"Stop it!" Ben laughed until his eyes watered.

Laura grinned. "That's enough kids! Our meal's going to burn!" She pointed her index finger at Ben "You're not allowed in the kitchen, is that clear? Thomas is making a pot pie and I'm baking a cake." Her face twisted as she admitted, "At least, I'm trying to."

Thomas released Ben with a contagious laugh, then headed back to the kitchen.

Still grinning, Ben picked himself up and was heading upstairs when the doorbell rang. He opened the door, only to find there was no-one there. A whiff of ice-cold air smacked him in the face. Tike scurried outside.

"Tike!" Ben called, grabbing his scarf and wrapping it around his ears and mouth as he followed the dog. Tike tailed a person who walked away hurriedly with hunched shoulders.

"Kimi!" Ben yelled, recognizing the long, black coat.

He ran after her, trying to ignore the biting cold. He reached her and touched her shoulder. "Kimi?" he said again.

Only then did she stop and look at him.

"Hi!" Ben said.

She hid her face behind her long bangs, seeming embarrassed at having been discovered. "Hi," she said shyly. "I didn't mean to disturb. I'll come by some other time."

"No, no, that's ok. Can we go inside, please? I'm freezing!" He stuffed his hands in his pockets.

She was obviously reluctant to accept, but she nodded and followed him back to the house. He took off his scarf, noticing that she didn't move from the front door even though he had closed it. She seemed to want to be able to head out again at the slightest chance.

"You weren't at school all week," Ben noted. "Have you been sick?"

She shook her head, her eyes hiding behind the strand of hair sticking out from under her black beanie. "I had to help my mom," she said vaguely. "She hasn't been feeling well."

"Oh, I'm sorry." An awkward silence fell over them, until he ventured, "Er…is there something we can do to help?"

She shook her head. "No, it's fine. It's just that, I was wondering if I could borrow your notes."

Ben's face brightened, finally understanding the reason for her visit. "Of course!" he smiled encouragingly. "Do you want to hang your coat here?"

She started taking it off when she noticed the nicely

laid table. Her eyes widened. "Oh! I didn't realize you were going to have dinner! Maybe I should go..."

At that moment, Laura stepped out of the kitchen. When she saw Kimi, she glanced at Ben in surprise.

He gestured towards the girl. "Mom, this is Kimi from my school..."

Laura's face broke into a smile. "Hi, Kimi. That's so sweet of you to come by for Ben's birthday!"

Ben and Kimi exchanged a lightning glance. Kimi's face went crimson. "I...I had no idea!" she stammered. "You should have told me it was your birthday," she scolded. "You obviously have plans. I'll come back another time..."

But Laura put her hands on her hips. "Now wait a minute! Ben hasn't had any school friends over since we arrived! Why don't you stay for dinner? We'd love to have you!"

"Mom!" Ben exclaimed, the blood rushing to his cheeks, then he refrained from saying anything more as he realized he didn't dislike the idea. He glanced at Kimi to see how she would react.

The girl resembled a small bird caught in a trap. Ben could see her brain scrambling for an excuse. "I don't know..." was all she came up with.

"I'll tell you what," Laura offered "Why don't you guys head on up and start your homework. You can think about it and decide later, Kimi. How's that sound?"

Kimi replied in a small voice, "Um, ok." She apparently liked the delayed decision better.

Ben smiled excitedly. "Yeah! Come on up! I need

help with the literature assignment."

Kimi hung up her jacket this time, though she kept her beanie hat on. "Why didn't you tell me it was your birthday?" she hissed as they climbed the stairs.

"Because you weren't at school, dummy!" he teased. Kimi punched him in the side and he laughed. When they reached the landing, he turned to her, saying, "Hey! How did you know where I lived?"

She shrugged. "Everybody knows where Thomas lives."

✳ ✳ ✳

Laura struggled with the icing pipe; the frosting she had made was too runny and oozed down her fingers instead of on the cake. She squealed when the doorbell rang again and stuffed the sweet goo into her mouth before it fell to the floor. As she opened the door with her sticky hands, she heard Kimi clambering down the stairs behind her.

A woman with waist-long, black hair stood in the dim light.

"Hi," the woman said. "I'm Maggie, Kimi's mother."

"Hi, nice to meet you. I'm Laura," she replied. "Sorry I can't shake your hand; mine are full of icing." She let Maggie in, suddenly realizing that there was a furious look on the woman's face. It was directed at Kimi.

"Kimimela!" Maggie said sharply. "Where have you been? I've been looking all over for you!"

"I was doing homework!" Kimi snapped. "I missed school, *remember?*"

"What's gotten into you? You don't go to people's houses on a whim like that! These people obviously have better things to do!" Maggie retorted.

"Fiiine!" Kimi said in exasperation as Ben joined the group. She grabbed her jacket, glaring at her mother. "Let's go, then!"

Thomas materialized out of the kitchen. "Maggie!" he bellowed. "Is that you? I don't believe it! It's been ages!" He rushed to the woman with his arms outstretched and a big smile, oblivious to the unfolding drama. He placed both hands gently on the woman's shoulders and kissed her on each cheek.

"This must be my lucky day!" he continued enthusiastically. "You won't believe what I'm making! I'm trying out your famous pot pie recipe and failing grandly at it! You're just the person I need! Please, please, help me. I need to know which herbs you use..." He chatted away, leading Maggie into the kitchen before she could object.

Laura, Ben and Kimi remained in the hallway, staring at each other uncomfortably.

Laura jumped into action. "Ben, grab an extra set of chairs. Kimi, could you add a couple of plates to the table, please? Dinner will be ready in five minutes, and we've got plenty of it!"

Everyone pretended nothing had happened only a

moment earlier. Kimi hung up her jacket once more, then helped Laura with the dishes while Ben brought two chairs from the upstairs bedrooms.

Aware that Thomas was trying to lighten the mood, Laura noticed he gave Maggie and Kimi no chance to leave the house. He kept Maggie in a constant conversation until, unexpectedly, they were all sitting at the table, admiring Thomas' steaming pot pie and Laura's fresh spinach salad.

Only Mesmo's seat was empty. Laura figured it was best to set a plate for him, explaining that her husband, Jack, was working late. Maggie accused Thomas of making Ben's dad work too late on the boy's birthday, to which Thomas replied that Jack had no reason to complain: he was working in the warm Canmore Air hangar while he himself had just come from a three-day trip way up in the Inuvialuit Region.

Laura glanced at Thomas in surprise, wondering what Thomas had been doing so far North of the Arctic Circle. She had become used to Thomas' frequent absences, as he was hired as a pilot to fly to remote locations. She hadn't realized he had to fly that far away and made a mental note to question him later. She stood up, saying she would bring something to drink for this special occasion.

In the kitchen, she took a bottle of red wine from a cabinet, opened it, then found three wine glasses for herself, Thomas and Maggie. When she turned around, Thomas was standing right behind her.

"Oh!" she gasped, almost dropping the bottle.

Thomas had a bleak look on his face which caught her off guard. "Not that!" he whispered urgently, taking the wine bottle away from her.

"Hey! What are you doing?" she objected.

Thomas put a finger to his lips, indicating she shouldn't speak so loudly.

Laura lowered her voice. "What going on?"

Thomas said in a quiet, serious voice, "Maggie can't handle alcohol."

Laura's eyes widened. Very slowly, she let out a long, "Oh!" Carefully, she placed the wine glasses back on the kitchen sink, then turned around to face him again. "I'm sorry," she breathed. "I had no idea."

Thomas nodded sadly. "Juice would be better," he said, then headed back to the dining room where she heard him say joyfully, "Who wants seconds?"

When Laura sat down again, Thomas was asking Maggie to tell them stories about the people of Canmore, most of whom she had known for years. Both Thomas and Maggie took turns telling funny stories about the neighbourhood, making them all laugh.

When it was time for dessert, Laura switched off the lights and brought in the cake she had baked for her son. They sang Happy Birthday, then Ben blew out the candles after Laura encouraged him to make a wish. When she switched on the lights again, Mesmo was standing in the kitchen doorway, startling them.

Recovering swiftly, Laura shouted, "Surprise!"

Ben said, "Hi, Dad!" with a crooked smile on his face.

Laura cleared her throat, then introduced him. "This is my husband, Jack." She turned to him, adding, "You made it home just in time for the cake, honey!" She moved a chair aside at the table so he could sit with them without having to shake Maggie and Kimi's hands. Laura presented the guests to him while she cut the cake.

Mesmo nodded to them, then turned his attention to Ben. "Happy birthday, Ben," he said, playing along. "There's a gift waiting for you in the yard."

Laura threw him a warning glance, but he ignored her.

"Really?" Ben said with genuine surprise.

Before Laura could react, Ben and Kimi were out of their chairs, dashing to the kitchen. The adults followed.

Laura heard Ben exclaim, "Wow!" as he opened the kitchen door and rushed out. Ignoring the freezing air, she spotted the gift immediately: a very well made, round igloo with a square opening.

"Terrific!" Kimi exclaimed.

Ben ran back, his eyes shining. Breathless with excitement, he said, "Thanks, Dad. I love it!"

Mesmo nodded. "I thought you would."

A smile crept on to Laura's face. She caught Mesmo's eye and mouthed, "Thank you."

* * *

Later that evening, Thomas insisted on driving Kimi and Maggie home so they wouldn't have to walk in the cold. Laura was stacking dishes in the dishwasher by the time he returned.

"Where's Mesmo?" Thomas asked.

"He's still outside." He'd been outside ever since the children had discovered the igloo.

Thomas headed for the wine bottle, pulled out the cork and filled up two wine glasses. He passed one to Laura and they gently clanked their glasses together.

"Here's to a not-too-messed-up-cake," Thomas said, winking at her.

Laura laughed. "Here's to a scrumptious pot pie."

They each took a sip out of their glasses.

"I had a good evening, Thomas!" Laura said earnestly. "I'm glad Kimi and Maggie decided to stay. It made Ben really happy. He needed some sense of normalcy."

Thomas nodded. "I needed that, too. I mostly avoid town folk. They're too nosy. But Maggie's ok."

Laura glanced at her wine glass thoughtfully. "Thank you for stopping me earlier. I had no idea Maggie had a drinking problem."

Thomas placed his glass on the kitchen counter and began cleaning a pot in the sink. "I don't think she was always like that, you know? Apparently, before her husband abandoned her, you wouldn't have recognized her. People say she was a hard worker. Her veterinary practice was the place to go if you had a sick animal. She'd take on a lot more work than she could handle because her good-for-nothing husband spent his days on the couch. I don't know what she saw in him. They say he was never satisfied. He always expected more of her and she would try to keep him happy." Thomas handed her a pot, which she dried with a kitchen towel, absorbed by his tale.

"Then one day he packed his bags, went out the door, and never came back. Maggie couldn't get over it. She felt it was her fault he'd left. She's been on a downward spiral ever since. She gave up on her practice, she's given up on being a mother to Kimi..." He paused, thinking, then added sadly, "Basically, she's given up on herself."

Placing the dry pot on the kitchen counter, she observed Thomas while he spoke. With some surprise in her voice, she said, "You have feelings for her...!"

Thomas handed her another pot, looking her straight in the eyes. "I do," he admitted. "I'm not ashamed of it. She's a wonderful woman! She's just forgotten it." He scrubbed a pan mechanically, lost in thought. "If only she would remember who she was, maybe I wouldn't be so invisible to her..."

Laura stared at him sadly, trying to find something comforting to say. Before she could reply, Thomas said half-jokingly, "What a sad pair we make, you and me!"

She stopped wiping the pot and frowned. "What do you mean?"

He stared at her in surprise. "Come now! You read

me like an open book, Laura. Don't think I haven't been reading you, too!" He rinsed the pan, shaking his head with half a smile on his face. "Me, in love with a woman who barely knows I exist. And you, in love with an extraterrestrial. For goodness sake!" he snorted. "It couldn't get more complicated than that!"

Laura had stopped drying the pot altogether, her mouth opened in protest, but when she realized he was onto her, her cheeks turned crimson, and she remained silent.

Thomas glanced at her and said gently, "There's nothing to be ashamed of. These aren't feelings you can control. They just kind of creep up on you until you can't shake them off again." He pulled the plug from the sink, then rested his hands against the side. "We've got to keep believing, Laura. Anything can happen. You never know…"

Laura stared at the window to an imaginary landscape outside. It was too dark to see anything, only the light from the kitchen and her own reflection on the windowpane. "Mesmo has to leave within four months," she said in a haunted voice.

Thomas frowned. "Why?"

"He said he must return to a place called Enceladus. If he doesn't make it there within four months, he'll be stuck here. He won't be able to go home, ever."

"Enceladus, Enceladus…" Thomas repeated as if trying to remember something. He grabbed his iPad from the kitchen table and Googled ENCELADUS.

Laura watched over his shoulder as the results

appeared on the screen. She scanned the articles, one which mentioned an Enceladus from Greek mythology. But what caught their attention were images on the right of the screen. They belonged to a ghostly, grey-white moon which, the description said, belonged to Saturn, the sixth planet of the solar system.

CHAPTER EIGHT

Northern Lights

After insisting that Thomas head up to bed, Laura finished putting things back in place. She switched off the kitchen lights, then sipped on her wine, enjoying a calm moment to herself. As her eyes grew accustomed to the dark, she began making out the landscape through the window. To her surprise, she could see quite far, and it wasn't until she bent over the counter that she realized the full moon was shining, illuminating the snow-white hillsides. The glimmering globe rested on top of the distant mountain range, ready to dip behind them and leave Canmore in complete darkness. As she observed the tranquil scenery, she noticed movement on top of the nearest hill. She squinted and stuck her forehead to the frosty windowpane to get a better look.

Two figures were silhouetted against the skyline.

Laura grabbed some dusty binoculars from the top of the fridge and glued them to her eyes. Soon, Mesmo came into view, tall and straight, while before him stood a much shorter woman with a thick parka, snow boots and snow trousers. Although her head was covered by a warm fur-lined cap, her long, black braids flowed from both sides of her neck to her waist. She had a long, straight nose, high cheekbones and slanted eyes. Her skin was creased from being out in the weather for many years.

The pair looked sufficiently uncommon to catch Laura's attention. She observed them for a long moment, attracted by their curious silhouettes and mysterious conversation.

Suddenly, both figures turned their faces in her direction and she was convinced they were looking straight at her. She shrank back, her heart beating fast. But then she straightened and frowned. *Why am I hiding?* She purposefully opened the kitchen door and glanced in their direction.

The woman bent and placed something on the snow, then turned and walked away in the opposite direction from the town. Mesmo remained where he was, standing still as a statue.

Laura went inside again, grabbed her jacket and snow boots, then headed out the back door. The cold was so intense she almost turned back. Yet Mesmo's simple brown jacket and relaxed stance played tricks on her mind, convincing her maybe it wasn't that cold after all.

She plodded forward, struggling to put one foot before the other as she sank knee-deep in the snow.

She was half-way there when Mesmo bent and placed his hand above the snow. A soft, blue light emanated from it, seeping through the surface to Laura's feet. The snow melted before her eyes, forming a solid path all the way up the hill. She joined him easily, finding that it wasn't as cold as she had expected. They stood next to each other, taking in the rolling white landscape covered by the starlit sky.

Laura glanced at her feet and found what looked like a deformed treble clef from a music partition. She picked it up: smaller than the palm of her hand, made from a heavy metal she couldn't identify.

She held it up to Mesmo quizzically.

"Will you keep that safe for me?" he asked.

She stared at the object again. "What is it?"

"Information," he said.

She frowned. "Who was that? The old woman you were talking to just now?"

"She is *Angakkuq²*, the Wise One from the North."

As usual, his answer left her with more questions, but something clicked in her mind. "From the North?" her mind whirled. "Did Thomas fly her over?"

Mesmo nodded. "Yes. I could not travel to meet her for obvious reasons, so she agreed to come. Thomas <u>picked her up at my req</u>uest."

---

² *Angakkuq* = shaman in Inuit.

"Why?" Laura asked, bursting with curiosity. "Why did you need to meet with her? Why do you need this object? Does it have to do with your mission?"

Mesmo stared at her. "Yes."

Laura waited in vain for more, but since he remained silent, she insisted, "Will you tell me why you came to Earth?"

He gazed away and she thought he might not answer. But then he said, "I came to assess the planet. My people have been doing so since before the beginning of the Human era, every two hundred Earth years. Seven Wise Ones report to us from different parts of the planet, from places you currently call Bolivia, Australia, Kenya, Polynesia, Norway, China and Northern Canada. I have met with six of them now. My last stop after Bolivia was going to be China, but then I came back here instead and was waylaid..."

Laura's eyes widened in amazement. "You've been to all those places?"

Mesmo nodded. "I have."

Laura needed a moment to let this revelation sink in. An uneasy feeling seeped into her mind. He had said something about assessing the planet, and, even though his people had supposedly been visiting the Earth for millions of years, she had to ask, "Are you going to...invade us?" She had seen enough science-fiction movies to nourish her imagination.

He took in the view again with his head turned, so she wasn't sure he had heard her. But then she thought she heard him mutter, "We cannot invade what is already ours."

"Excuse m...?" she began, her voice freezing as she caught a movement in the sky out of the corner of her eye. Her head shot up in surprise.

The moon had dipped behind the mountains, leaving only the stars to light the white surroundings. But then the movement came again. It was a river of bluish-green light that illuminated the night sky, swaying in total silence like a kaleidoscope from one end of the firmament to the other. It transformed from a small stream to a wide mantle that covered them, flowing and twirling smoothly over their heads.

"Aurora borealis," Mesmo whispered.

Laura's voice was lost in her throat. When she found it again, she echoed his words. "Yes. It's the Northern Lights!"

They watched in awe as the solar wind, which hit the Earth's atmosphere, transformed into a swirling display of colours, ranging from green, to blue, to purple. Its magnificence left Laura speechless. She had never seen the Earth put on such an overwhelming show. She felt tiny before such celestial power. They stood side by side as though they were the only beings alive in this quiet world, and the sky celebrated their existence.

Her eyes slid back to Mesmo. "You know I love you, don't you?" she breathed, the words leaving her mouth in such a natural way, she did not even try to stop them.

He turned to face her. Although covered with

shadows, his brows knit together slightly. Was it from sadness? Or disappointment? He opened his mouth to speak, but she interrupted before he could.

"Don't!" she said. Then, more gently, "You don't have to say anything. I've been fighting this feeling for the longest time. There's nothing I can do about it. It's the simple truth and I have to learn to live with it."

She studied his handsome face. "I don't expect anything from you, Mesmo. I know your people won't allow you to love again..." She sucked in air. "...which is something I will never understand...but I know you have to leave. And I promise I will do everything in my power to help you get back home." Her eyes clouded. She breathed deeply and turned to face the landscape so he wouldn't see her tears.

The Northern Lights faded away slowly, leaving place for the stars and distant, incoming clouds. A freezing wind picked up around them, seeping through their invisible cocoon.

"Laura," he said.

She struggled to look at him, not wanting him to see her so vulnerable. When she faced him, she noticed that his eyes were sparkling. Was he crying, too?

He stated in a clear voice, "I cannot love you."

They held each other's gaze for the longest moment, like an invisible bond drawing them together. Then, without warning, he closed his tired eyes and disappeared.

Laura gasped at the sudden, cold void before her.

The wind whipped at her face, freezing her ears and nose. With a heavy heart, she abandoned the hilltop and trudged back to the house, holding the alien object tightly. And all the while, she pondered the hidden meaning behind Mesmo's words, when he had purposefully said, "I *cannot* love you," instead of "I *do not* love you."

In a high-rise of Phoenix City, sprawled in the Arizona desert, a stocky man typed a password on his laptop. The screen wavered before revealing black-and-white images. The camera that filmed the images was placed in the top corner of a bare room. A hospital bed was the only furniture. A tall man lay on it.

The man adjusted his Gucci glasses before using the mouse on his laptop to zoom in on the sleeping man's face, then waited expectantly. Soon, the man's eyes fluttered open. He remained lying still for some time before pushing himself up into a sitting position with difficulty. Even on the black-and-white image, his white hair contrasted with his darker tan and eyes. After remaining that way for several minutes, the subject being watched so intently got off the bed, then took a few paces around the room, rubbing his face with his hands.

He seemed to notice a food tray that had been shoved under the only door in the room and stared at it for some time, before reaching down to pick it up. He placed the tray on the bed and poked unenthusiastically at its contents. Finally, he picked up the hamburger and took a small bite.

A distant voice came through the computer. "Boss, are you watching this?"

The stocky man knitted his thick black and grey eyebrows, unhappy at the interruption. "Of course, I am!" he said icily. "The question is, what am I to make of it?"

The voice said neutrally, "He's getting better. Whatever it is he's doing during his blackouts is working. We held off the feeding tube as long as we could. The invasive procedure could have set his heart racing again. So this is a good sign."

"Is it?" The green-eyed man asked as the air conditioning started blowing through his curly black and grey hair. "I don't trust him," he stated. "For all we know, these blackouts could be his way of reaching out for help. We don't know what he's capable of."

There was a silence at the other end, then the contact said, "There's not much we can do except monitor him until you return." There was a pause, then the voice asked, "How's it going on your end, Boss?"

The man sitting in the Phoenix office stretched out the fingers of his left hand which held a golden ring on the index finger. "We're good for now," he said. "Our partners will hold off. But I must get answers when I return or things will get ugly."

The far away contact asked carefully, "What if he

doesn't have answers?"

The stocky man snapped, "Of course he has answers! You don't cross half the universe without that type of knowledge! Mark my words: that alien has the information I need, and he will give it to me!"

CHAPTER NINE

Dakhona

Wes and Tyler ambushed them on a Monday afternoon in early February. By the time Christmas break had come and gone, Ben and Kimi had forged a strong friendship and he had long since grown accustomed to walking home with her instead of taking the bus. Sometimes she would drop by Thomas' house so they could do their homework together, or they would take Tike for a long walk. Ben knew he was clinging on to Kimi, first and foremost because he enjoyed her company, but also because she kept both his feet on the ground. With her, Ben remembered to be a student, a friend, and, basically, an ordinary boy going about his normal teen business.

It happened just as they reached the school field bordered by a group of pine trees.

"Aargh!" Ben yelled when a freezing snowball smacked him in the back of his neck. He barely had time to turn to search for the culprit, when Kimi's backpack was struck by another snowball. They heard laughter and spotted Wes and Tyler peeking out from behind the trees.

"Take cover!" Kimi shouted as they were pelted by another batch of snowballs.

They searched for safety but found none, so they scooped up snow themselves and aimed at the two hidden boys. But their efforts were useless; Wes and Tyler had the advantage of cover and a stack of ammunition.

Kimi howled at the top of her voice and charged towards the attackers. The two boys threw their remaining snowballs at her until she fell headfirst into the snow. They hooted with laughter.

"Whoa!" Tyler shouted when he saw Kimi getting up again.

"She's crazy! Run for it!" Wes yelled.

The boys made their escape, laughing loudly.

Ben caught up with Kimi. "Are you ok?" he asked, unable to wipe a big grin from his face when he saw her snow-covered face.

"What?" she retorted. "I scared them off, didn't I?" She grinned at him as he reached for her hand to pull her upright. She brushed the snow from her flushed cheeks.

They headed off again, checking their surroundings for another attack. Once they had made it safely to the street, Ben invited Kimi over for some hot chocolate, which she accepted gladly. She was much more at ease in

Thomas' house since Ben's birthday dinner three months earlier, and clearly enjoyed his and Tike's company. She did not seem in a hurry to go home anymore.

They sipped on the hot liquid in Ben's room. He tapped a pen on his notebook, trying to figure out a math problem, while Kimi lay on her stomach, scratching Tike's head.

"Ben," she said. "How come Tike can't bark?"

Stiffening slightly, Ben answered, "He was in an accident. I think the shock damaged his vocal chords."

"Really?" Kimi exclaimed, placing her weight on her elbows to look at him better. "I wonder what type of accident it was. I've never heard of anything like it before."

Ben pretended to concentrate very hard on his math book. Staring at the numbers, he said deftly, "How come your mom calls you Kimimela?"

Kimi rolled on her back, staring at the ceiling. She blew the side bangs out of her eyes, then said, resigned, "It's a Native name. It means 'butterfly.'" After a pause, she added, "My mother's name is Magaskawee. She is of Dakhona First Nation. She left the reservation when she married my dad."

Ben considered her reply. "So you're First Nation, too?"

Kimi lifted her eyes in annoyance. "Only half."

"That's really cool!"

Kimi stood up suddenly. "No, it's not!" she burst out, startling him. "Why does everybody always say that? I hate being First Nation! It sucks!" She grabbed her backpack and stormed out of the room, leaving Ben gaping.

* * *

Kimi was absent the following two days. Ben found himself deeply worried. He wondered how he had managed to upset her; for the life of him he couldn't figure out what had set her off. He walked home, lost in thought, completely forgetting about Wes and Tyler until it was too late.

Cries of war surrounded him. He ducked with a yelp just as the two boys appeared out of nowhere and pounded him with snow bullets.

Not this time!

He plunged his hands in the snow and shoved it at them as fast as he could. Soon the three of them were flopping around like fish out of water, their arms flailing as they urgently reached for more ammunition to defend themselves. By the time they were finished, Ben lay flat on his back, laughing and hurting at the same time.

"Ah, this is no fun!" Wes said, grinning. "Two against one! Where's that scardycat girlfriend of yours, Ben?"

Ben launched a handful of snow at him but Wes avoided it as he laughed.

"See ya!" Tyler yelled, and the two boys scampered away, pushing at each other playfully.

Ben remained on his back, catching his breath. A

shadow hovered above his face and Mesmo came into view.

"Did those boys hurt you?" he asked.

"Nah," Ben replied as he got himself off the ground and brushed snow away from his jacket. "I just wish I could get back at them, is all."

They watched as the two boys walked away. Mesmo bent suddenly and placed his hands in the snow. A flash of blue emanated from them, shooting through the white ground towards a pine tree next to the boys. Ben swore the tree shivered. A mound of snow released from the branches right on to the boys' heads. They yelled in shock as they were buried under a small heap.

Ben's eyes bulged at the sight. He glanced in disbelief at Mesmo, then at the boys, then back at Mesmo.

You've got to be kidding me!

He fell over in a guffaw of laughter.

Wes and Tyler shouted at him angrily, their honour in shambles, as they struggled to get out of the mess. They hurried away, leaning on to each other, while Ben laughed his heart out.

"Did you *see* that?" he gasped, trying to catch his breath. "That was *awesome!*"

Mesmo stared at him quizzically. "You're doing that thing again," he noted.

Ben wiped his eyes. "What thing?"

"You're laughing and crying at the same time."

That only set Ben off again. "Oh boy, you have a lot to learn! Remind me to teach you about jokes some time."

He bent to pick up his backpack, which he had dropped on the field before the attack happened. "Come on, let's get out of here." He peeked over his shoulder to make sure Mesmo was heading off with his back turned. He straightened, holding a huge snowball in his hands. "Timber!" he yelled, throwing the big snowball at Mesmo. But it went right through the alien and landed in a useless heap on the other side.

Mesmo stopped in his tracks, then turned slowly, throwing Ben a cheeky look.

"Uh-oh!" Ben moaned, slapping his gloved hand on his forehead.

How could I forget?

Ben turned to make a run for it when what felt like a truckload of snow crashed on top of him from a nearby tree, nailing him to the ground. He spluttered and coughed the snow out of his mouth.

Mesmo bent over him with his hands on his knees. Ben saw the alien grin. "Was that a good joke?" he asked.

Ben groaned in surrender. "Not fair."

Mesmo placed a hand on the mound of snow to melt it so that Ben could free himself. Smiling, the alien teased, "You have the wrong skill, my friend."

"Nothing!" High Inspector Tremblay hit his desk

with his fist. A stack of files slid off, crashing in a messy heap on the floor, while an expensive-looking pen did a somersault.

The sturdy middle-aged man with a perm-pressed suit grabbed the one file that was still placed on his desk and pointed it threateningly at the two men standing before him. "For heaven's sake, we are the CSIS, one of the most respected agencies in Canada. And you dare come to me with…" he waved the file in their faces, "…nothing!"

He paced up-and-down the length of the desk while Hao and Connelly stood before him, weathering the storm.

"What do I care if you picked up a homeless guy off the streets of Chilliwack? What do I care if he ran off with that woman, Laura Archer? It's the little green men I want! Where are they? Not a shred of hair! Not a single fingerprint! My meeting with the Minister of Defense is scheduled next week. What do you expect me to tell her?' The Americans and the Chinese think we're incapable! We're the laughing stock of the international secret services! If you don't deliver pronto, this country will lose control of the biggest case in the history of the planet!"

The muscles on the side of his neck tensed. "You have one week, gentlemen! One week to uncover the little green men! If I go down after that, I'm taking you down with me!"

Hao waited for the blink of an eye before he ventured to speak, "Yes, Sir!" He understood full well that he could be jobless within seven days.

With a visibly superhuman effort to calm himself, the High Inspector barked, "Dismissed!"

Immediately, Hao and Connelly exited the modern office. Once they were in the hallway, Hao said, "We're back at square one. We've got to find that plane!"

"Yes," Connelly agreed. "And while you do that, I'll widen the perimeter for the facial recognition programs."

"Excuse me?" Hao retorted with an offended tone, stopping in his tracks to face Connelly. "That's searching for a needle in a haystack. Besides, we already have a team accessing public cameras. That plane is our best bet, and I need you on it!"

"Your plane search doesn't require a big workforce. Problem is, your fugitives could be miles away from the plane's landing location by now. Public cameras are our best bet. Trust me, I know what I'm doing."

Hao stepped an inch from Connelly's face and pointed a finger at him. The other did not budge at the menacing gesture. "Listen here, wonder boy. I don't like you. Never have. Never will. But I run the show around here, and when I give you an order, you follow it. I didn't get to where I am by dawdling in front of TV screens all day. If you don't believe me, you can check my track record. Just see how many criminals I've put behind bars. I did my homework and had a look at *your* record. Guess how many you've caught during your very long small-town police career? None! Zilch! Nada! So when I tell you I need you to work on finding that plane, you get on board, or I'll have you distributing parking tickets in a heartbeat.

Do I make myself clear?"

Invisible static filled the narrow space between them. Connelly's mouth twitched as he glared back at Hao with cold, impenetrable eyes.

"Yes, Sir," the bald man replied stiffly, though Hao could almost touch the smouldering anger emanating from his colleague.

CHAPTER TEN

Ice

"Ben, have you seen Kimi lately?" Ms. Evans asked.

Ben shook his head.

Ms. Evans' shoulders sagged. "I was hoping she would be in today. You know the civics exam is next Friday, right? I'd like her to be ready for it."

Ben offered, "I can go by her house later and give her a copy of my notes."

Ms. Evans smiled. "Well, if it's not too much trouble..." She handed him some photocopies. "She should study these as well."

Ben took the documents and nodded when she thanked him. As he crossed the school field, he remained on the lookout for Wes and Tyler, but the two had clearly learned their lesson because they were nowhere in sight.

He walked several blocks, then had to backtrack when he realized he had taken a wrong turn. Finally, he found a door with a veterinary sign on it that he took to be the front of Kimi's house. He pressed the doorbell, which chimed loudly inside.

A distraught voice called, "Kimimela?" It was followed by shuffling sounds and the outline of a woman appeared behind the hazy doorframe. "Kimimela?" the woman's voice came again as she opened the door. She stiffened at the sight of Ben.

Ben stared at the woman in surprise. He barely recognized Kimi's mother: her hair was a mess, a night robe fell loosely over her crumpled pyjamas which were unevenly buttoned up, and there were deep bags under her hazy eyes.

Maggie brushed away at her uncombed hair with the tips of her fingers. "Hi, Ben," she greeted him shakily, her breath smelling foul. "I thought you were Kimimela."

"Hi," Ben said awkwardly.

Maggie attempted to straighten her clothes unsuccessfully. "Kimi's not here. We had a fight this morning. It's not easy for her, you know, taking care of her sick mama. I haven't been very well, you see..." She seemed to remember something. "Oh, were you here about the crow? I released it a month ago. I'm sorry, I should have told you..."

Ben shook his head. "No, no, it's ok. I was just bringing some notes for Kimi. We have an exam next Friday." He pulled out Ms. Evan's photocopies from his backpack and handed them to her.

Maggie's lower lip began to tremble. "You're a good friend, Ben," she said gratefully. "She desperately needs one."

Ben felt sorry for her. She had shown a witty spirit on the evening of his birthday, telling colourful tales about the region with great enthusiasm. Not so today, however. He thought of his friend with a pang of sadness, realizing how hard it must be for Kimi to live with a mother in this state. He cleared his throat. "Well, please tell Kimi I said hi, and to let me know if she needs anything."

He took a step back, but Maggie reached out her hand as if to hold him back. "Wait! Please, Ben. Would you mind looking for her? I'm really worried. I haven't seen her since breakfast."

"Sure," he said. He noted her distressed face and added more firmly, "Yes, of course! Don't worry. I'll find her and tell her to come home." He waved and headed down the street.

Maggie shouted after him, "Check the lake! She likes to go there when she needs to be by herself."

Ben nodded and jogged off with Tike.

The air brushed cold against his skin. The sky was low and grey, reflecting on the fresh, even snow that had fallen that morning. There was no sign of spring, yet. Ben hunched deep into his thick coat, covering his mouth with his scarf, his toque low over his ears. Tike wore a red dog coat, which Kimi had given him for Christmas. They reached the end of an alley and crossed into a large park. It was a bleak, empty landscape, dotted with trees. In the middle stood a small lake bordered by a low hill to the left. In this white world, Ben easily spotted Kimi's black snow coat from afar. There was no-one else in sight as she slid elegantly over the ice. He read the sign at the edge of the lake: WARNING. THIN ICE. ICE SKATING PROHIBITED.

Ben looked from the warning sign to the girl who paid no heed to it. Kimi wore her usual black snow trousers, knee-length jacket and military-style boots. But for once, she did not have her beanie hat on. Instead, her dark hair fell freely to her waist, straight and shiny. Ben realized he had never seen it loose before. He found himself mesmerized by the way it changed her face. She was no longer hiding behind her long bangs, which she had pulled back behind her ear. He could see her pixie eyes and nose and noted with a blush that she was very pretty.

"What are you waiting for?" Kimi interrupted his thoughts. She half-walked, half-slid to the middle of the lake, though she didn't get far without ice skates.

Ben glanced at the sign again. He said loudly, "I think you should come off the ice. Your mom sent me to find you. She's worried."

"Ha!" the girl snorted. "Is she, now? Or did she need somebody to pour her a drink because she can't even stand on her own two feet anymore? Yeah, she drinks, did you know that?" She shot him a glance.

"I..." he began, embarassed, but he could tell she

wasn't even listening to him.

"I'm surprised you didn't know that. Everybody in town knows the vet lady who drinks! Now you know, too. A regular Canmore citizen, you are!"

Ben, who hadn't expected this outburst, felt anger swelling as she spoke. "Don't talk like that!"

"I'll stop if you come on over. I dare you! Or are you scared?" she taunted.

Ben was so upset by her tone that he stepped onto the ice without thinking. Immediately, Tike jumped before him, barring his teeth.

Danger!

Ben stared at his dog in surprise but came back to his senses. He took his foot off the icy surface.

"Oh, poor dear. He's s-o-o scared!" Kimi mocked, laughing snidely.

"Knock it off, Kimi! Get off the ice. It's dangerous!"

She shrugged and ignored him, skating further away.

"Come on, Kimi. Why are you doing this?"

She whirled around, her face flushed with anger. "Do you know why my dad left us?" she yelled.

Ben lifted his arms helplessly, then shook his head, all the while searching the park in the hopes an adult would come by and talk some sense into the girl.

"He married my mom because she is pure-blooded Dakhona. The lazy bastard thought he'd get tax privileges by marrying a First Nation woman and grow stinking rich. Then, when he realized he'd never get his way, he abandoned us," she retorted. "He left me! My dad left me because I'm First Nation!" She was standing in the middle of the lake, shaking. "He left me because I'm a freak!"

Her words hit home more than Ben cared to admit. "No, you're not! Don't say stupid things like that!"

"Look who's talking!" she yelled at him. "You have the perfect dad, the perfect mom, the perfect family! What would you know about being different?"

A huge lump surged in his throat.

You have no idea!

He was about to retort, then gritted his teeth and balled his fists instead. He breathed heavily through his nose several times, then whirled around and stomped off.

"Hey, Ben!" Kimi shouted. "What..."

Her voice turned into a shriek as the ice broke. It made a horrible cracking sound through the lake. By the time Ben turned to face her again, she was already submerged, her hand sticking out like a final farewell.

"Kimi!" he screamed.

He ran back to the edge of the lake, placing a foot on the ice, but it went right through, filling his boot with icy water. He gasped and pulled back. He went up and down the lake, desperately searching for a way to reach his friend, but all he could see were round ripples on the surface where the ice had broken.

Over here!

Tike had scampered to the right of the lake and was carefully testing the ice. The dog lifted his head, his tongue lolling. It was more than instinct that told Ben his dog had found a safe spot to cross. Sure enough, this time the ice felt firm, for it did not crack or wobble under his feet.

Kimi resurfaced with a loud gasp. Her arms flailed in panic, searching in vain for something to hold on to. But the ice was crumbling and Ben could picture her big army boots dragging her down.

"Kimi!" Ben yelled urgently. "Hang on! I'm coming!"

Just as he threw his thick jacket off his shoulders, Mesmo appeared on the opposite side of the lake, the part bordered by the small hill. Ben hadn't reached the middle yet when Kimi sank again.

"No!" he shouted, tearing at his scarf. The freezing wind pierced through his sweater, but he took no notice. His panicked breath came up in steam before his eyes as he reached the broken ice and stared into the dark water.

Mesmo had already recognized the situation. He walked straight into the lake, plunging his hands into it. Then he stared at Ben and nodded urgently.

Ben understood.

I have to go in!

Without a second thought for his own safety, Ben took a big gulp of air and dove into the water. He yelled behind his closed mouth, expecting a heart-stopping cold. Darkness submerged him, yet as his skin tingled at the contact with the water, he realized he did not freeze up like he had expected to. He let himself float under the lake, blinking his eyes open, while bubbles lifted around him.

His senses told him that the water was comfortably

warm. He could see some feet before him; an eerie blue light filtered to the depth. His heartbeat slowed, and he became confident that he could search for Kimi safely. He swam up, breaking the surface, and gasped for breath. The freezing air entered his lungs and droplets of water froze in his hair, yet his immersed body remained warm.

After taking another deep breath of air and checking that Mesmo was still there, Ben plunged down again. He swam in the semi-darkness, the white ice hung ominously above him and rays of soft blue light illuminated the bottom. His lungs were about to burst when he spotted Kimi some way ahead, her boots dragging her down, her arms reaching upwards, her long hair spread like a fan around her head; her eyes were closed as if she were sleeping peacefully.

He had to go up for air again, then immediately swam towards her again. He reached out for her hand and pulled with all his might. She was heavier than he expected because of her layers of clothing, but he would not give up. He could see the broken ice above him. If only he could pull her up to catch a breath. Her hand slipped and she started to sink again. He shouted in panic behind his closed mouth, then swam to catch her again. This time he grabbed her under the armpits and kicked upwards.

The surface was so close now. His throat burst with pain as he fought not to open his mouth just yet. He reached out his hand and his fingers closed onto the edge of the ice. It was enough to help him heave both of them up. They broke the surface and he opened his mouth to let in a gulp of freezing air, which cut through his throat and lungs. He gasped in pain, swallowing water in the process. Struggling to hang on to the slippery ice, he spluttered and fought to keep Kimi's head up and out.

He blinked the moisture out of his eyes, strove to catch his bearings, and spotted Tike running up-and-down the side of the broken ice. Ben followed him, pulling himself by holding on to the crumbling side, trying to ignore the contrast in temperature above and below the ice.

Painstakingly, he made it to the shore, to the exact spot where he had been standing moments ago. In a last, exhausting effort, he dragged himself and Kimi out, their clothes heavy with water.

A heartwrenching cry came from behind him. He turned to find a woman entering the park. His legs gave way in numbness and he tumbled to the ground as Maggie and Mesmo rushed up to them.

"Kimi!" Maggie yelled in anguish. She threw herself on the ground next to her daughter, patting her on the cheek. "She's not breathing! Oh God! She's not breathing!"

Ben rolled over in shock, coming face to face with Kimi. The girl's lips were blue, her skin was as pale as a ghost, and not a hint of a heartbeat appeared on her skin.

"Kimi! Kimi!" Maggie cried, shaking her by the shoulders. She frantically performed CPR, pressing with the knuckles of her hands on the girl's chest, then applying mouth-to-mouth resuscitation. She did this several times but was so distraught that she lost energy fast. She sobbed in despair. "Kimimela! My butterfly! Come back to me!" Her pleading eyes found Ben's own. "This can't be happening! Please, help me!"

Ben hadn't realized that he was sobbing. His chin quivered with cold, his wet clothes covered his body with an icy layer, and he could not feel his hands. Yet all he noticed was the heavy feeling in the pit of his stomach. His eyes fell on Mesmo, begging the alien wordlessly.

Mesmo stared from Ben to Kimi with calm interest. He leaned forward, frowning, then placed his hands two inches above the girl. A faint, bluish light emanated from them, causing Maggie to catch her breath. As the alien's hands floated above Kimi's chest, he said, "I will try to extract the water. But I can't guarantee anything." He gazed at Ben as if sending him a silent message.

"What are you doing? Leave her alone!" Maggie gasped.

"It's ok-k! T-trust h-him," Ben stuttered through shivering lips.

Slowly, Mesmo's hands moved upwards from Kimi's stomach to her chest, then up to her throat and her mouth. A stream of water appeared at the corner of Kimi's lips like a snake. It flowed to the ground before turning into a small geyser as the warm liquid was drawn from her body.

Maggie grabbed her daughter by the shoulder and shook her. "Kimi! Come back to me! Kimi!"

The girl made a gurgling sound, then suddenly her

body heaved to the side as she coughed up more liquid.

Maggie cried in jubilation, while Ben fell back into the snow, an immense sense of relief washing over him. Kimi's eyes fluttered open and she blinked in confusion. Maggie brushed away her hair which was littered with icy droplets.

The girl caught her bearings. "*Iná...*" she began, her face crumpling. "I didn't mean..." she sobbed, unable to finish the phrase.

Her mother shushed her as she held her in her arms.

When she could speak again, Kimi whispered with an emotion-filled voice, "*Iná*, are you going to abandon me, too?"

Maggie's eyes widened. She took her daughter's face in her hands, then placed her forehead on the girl's own. With great determination, she answered, "Never!" She looked deep into Kimi's eyes. "I know I am lost, Kimimela, but I will find my way back to you! I promise!" She spoke words in a language Ben could not understand as mother and daughter hugged each other and sobbed.

"Benjamin!" Mesmo whispered urgently.

Out of the corner of his eye, Ben saw the alien disappear, while outside the park, two ambulances pulled up, followed closely by a police car. Paramedics swiftly pulled out stretchers from the back, then rushed over to them.

Ben reacted too late. He tried to get up, but his legs wouldn't cooperate. One paramedic covered him with a blanket, then a second one arrived, and they heaved him up with the intent of placing him on the stretcher.

"N-n-o!" Ben protested, realizing at the same time that he was paralyzed with cold. "N-no hosp-pital!" he stuttered as he struggled to roll off the stretcher. He could see the police officers getting out of their car and heading his way.

The first paramedic flashed a small light in his eyes. "What's your name, son?"

"B-Benjamin A-Archer," Ben said automatically, then caught himself. "A-Anderson! I mean B-ben And-derson!" He tried to get off the stretcher again.

The paramedic eyed him worriedly, then took his arm and gave him a swift injection. "You're in shock," he said calmly. "You're suffering from hypothermia, son. Don't worry, you'll be fine. Just try to relax, ok?"

Ben saw Kimi being taken away on the second stretcher. "No b-blood s-sample!" he managed to utter as he grabbed on to the paramedic's coat. But his fingers had lost their strength and his head swam as he felt himself fall into an induced slumber.

They'll find out!

CHAPTER ELEVEN

The War of the Kins

Laura Archer's forehead creased with worry over her tired, green eyes as she stared at her sleeping son. Her ash-brown hair was tied in a quick bun, and she bit her lip as she waited for Ben to show signs of waking. She stroked his hair away from his forehead. The boy did not stir but remained in a deep, repairing sleep. She followed the contour of his young face, which had lost its toddler roundness and showed hints of what he would look like as a man. It was only a matter of time before he would be taller than her.

"Laura," someone called softly behind her.

She turned to find Thomas in the doorway. He held the door open to let in a doctor of lanky stature and military-short, grey hair.

Thomas presented him. "This is Dr. Paul Hughes. He is President and CEO of the Canmore General Hospital." Then he added meaningfully, "He is also a faithful Canmore Air client."

Dr. Hughes and Laura shook hands. "That's right," the former said, smiling. "Thomas regularly flies me to conferences and remote locations across the province. I don't know what I'd do without him."

Thomas took over. "Dr. Hughes was kind enough to offer to check up on Ben himself."

Dr. Hughes held Laura's gaze, then said with sincerity, "I came to reassure you that Ben's welfare is our greatest concern, Ms. Anderson. The Canmore General Hospital will do everything to make his stay comfortable. But I must warn you that your son's heroic act may already have spread like wildfire. We will contain this story as best we can. I have instructed my staff personally to turn away any curious reporters. As a minor, Ben has the right to privacy and his name may not be shared without your strict consent."

Laura felt a huge weight lift from her shoulders. "Thank you. We don't want to become tabloid gossip. I really appreciate your discretion."

Dr. Hughes nodded. "You can count on it. Ben only suffers from mild hypothermia, which is quite astounding considering the time he spent in that freezing lake. I could dismiss him now, but encourage you to stay the night so we can monitor him. Physically, he will be back to his old self by tomorrow, though, emotionally, he may be a little shook up." He took out a card from an inside pocket and handed it to Laura. "Here's my card. Call me any time if you notice anything unusual. It will be my pleasure to help out a local hero. You can be proud of him!"

Laura gave him a weak smile as they shook hands again. As soon as the doctor left, Laura glanced at Thomas. "What do you think?" she asked in a low voice.

Thomas pursed his lips. "I think we should wait. We'll know by tomorrow if the media caught wind of this." He paused, before adding tensely, "But if they do, it could mean trouble..."

✳ ✳ ✳

Laura dozed off in an uncomfortable armchair by Ben's bed. She half-sat, half-lay with her head resting on her arm, her legs folded against her. She felt a soft whisp of air on her cheeks and blinked, only to find Mesmo kneeling before her, studying her face. She breathed deeply through her nose and stretched her cramped muscles.

"How long have you been here?" she asked, yawning. She checked that Ben was sleeping.

"A while," he replied, still staring at her. He pointed at Ben. "How is he?"

"The doctor says he'll be fine by morning," Laura said. She noticed his olive-coloured skin. "You look better," she observed.

Mesmo stared at his hands, then said, "I'm eating." He looked at her with his deep honey-brown eyes again, then added with a small smile, "At least, I am trying to."

Laura reached for his face, then followed the contour of his cheek with her hand. She marvelled at how real he looked from so close up. She could see every strand of hair of his brow, the texture of his skin, the detail of his iris. The thought that he was only an illusion when he seemed to be standing before her in flesh and bone was excruciating. She pulled her hand away and held on to the jacket that she had covered herself with to keep warm, never taking her eyes off him. After a silence, she said softly, "Tell me about your wife."

Mesmo sat on the floor next to her, leaning his arms on his bent knees. "Her name was Sila," he said. "She was beautiful and strong. She was highly regarded in her skill— one of the best. She insisted on keeping her hair short. She said it made it easier for her to shift." He smiled. "She would toy with me and change into amazing beings, but I would always find her in the crowd. It was her expression, you see. No matter who she shifted into, her mouth always made a funny smile, like this..." One corner of his mouth twisted upwards slightly.

Laura frowned as he spoke. "Wait a minute," she interrupted. "You said she could shift. Do you mean shapeshift? Like Bordock?"

Mesmo shook his head. "No, not like Bordock. Bordock was not born with a skill." His eyes darkened. "So he took hers." He wrung his hands together. "She did not survive."

A shiver crept up Laura's spine as she straightened in the chair. "What? Are you saying that Bordock forcefully took Sila's shapeshifting skill? Why would he do such a terrible thing?"

Mesmo sighed. "I will tell you why." He held her gaze the whole time he spoke. "My people are called the Toreq. We have spread into the Universe for billions of years and are accustomed to meeting new species and interacting with them. We respect their growth and search for identity and strive to maintain a balance between helping out and interfering as little as possible. The Toreq have created many alliances and trade fairly, though mostly we are satisfied with our home planet and strive to maintain a healthy balance on it.

"Many generations ago, the Toreq discovered a new species who called themselves the A'munh. We were astounded by their likeness to us, though they did not possess highly developed skills like ours. Still, we took a liking to them, and them to us. We felt as if we'd found distant cousins and were no longer alone in the darkness. We accepted them into our lives; they settled in our cities, in our homes, and made their way up to the ring of decision makers of our civilization. They, in turn, accepted us in the same way."

He paused. "By the time we realized they were not what they seemed, it was too late. They had infiltrated us to the highest ranks; they had blended into our families.

We had been blinded by our joy at finding a kindred species."

"Why?" Laura frowned, fascinated. "What did they do?"

"The A'munh were jealous of our skills and of our peaceful, balanced lives. They were impatient and wanted to reach the same results without understanding that only respect and long-term dedication over time could bring them our affluence. Things went from bad to worse and in their haste to get their hands on what we had, they began to exterminate us from within our very ranks. It took a while for us to realize what was happening. We could not comprehend that our brothers could turn against us like that. But too much jealousy had crept into their hearts and they began to scar the land and snatch things with greed. In spite of all our negotiation efforts, we were not able to avoid the Great War of the Kins."

"Both our people ended up broken and barely surviving. Yet the Toreq prevailed. In one of the most painful and shameful acts of our history, we extracted the remaining A'munh from our cities and banished them by force. This happened countless generations ago and we have grown strong again since then. We have not forgotten our past and have grown wiser than before."

He paused long enough to make Laura squirm, then stared away as he continued to speak. "It has come to light recently that some A'munh managed to remain hidden among us. The majority of my people live in ignorance of this danger, though a small group of us has become aware that dissidents exist. The A'munh survivors must have found out that I knew of them. That is why they sent a soldier to silence my family and me. And what better way to do that than far away from home?"

"Bordock?" Laura breathed.

Mesmo nodded.

She closed her eyes. How was it possible that she and her son had got caught up in this mess? She thought of Ben and her skin crawled. Her son had one of these alien skills now.

Mesmo must have noticed her face going pale, because he said, "You see, now, why I do not tell you much? I don't mean to frighten you."

She breathed in shakily, then leaned forward with determination. "There is only one thing I will ask of you."

Mesmo waited expectantly.

"Keep Bordock away from my son!"

CHAPTER TWELVE

Viral

Ben was cleared from hospital the next day, though he found out that Kimi had to remain there as she had contracted pneumonia and had to be put on antibiotics. She was reacting well to them, however, and doctors were counting on a speedy recovery.

Ben, Laura, Thomas and Mesmo spent the rest of the weekend at home, flipping through TV channels and radio stations to make sure there were no reports of the incident at the lake. Thomas said that he only heard a quick mention of it on a local radio station, but the conversation revolved more around the danger of people ignoring warning signs near frozen lakes or ice skating on their own.

By Monday morning, Laura told Ben that she had

spoken to Dr. Hughes, who confirmed that his staff had successfully snuffed out the story with curious reporters and that he had dealt with the police himself. She and Thomas decided it was safe to go about their usual activities. So, Laura headed to Tim Hortons, while Thomas dropped Ben off at school.

Alice, Joelle and Kimberly, the three popular girls of his class, were the only ones still removing their snow gear and rearranging their hair in front of his classroom when he arrived. While he hurriedly took off his toque and gloves, Kimberly turned to him and said shyly, "Hi, Ben."

"Uh, hi," Ben replied, taken aback by the greeting. She had never directed a single word at him before. He realized that all three were looking at him with bambi eyes and smiles that he could not interpret. Ben blushed and concentrated on removing his snow boots.

As he hung up his jacket, a sixth grader slapped him on the back. "Thumbs up, dude," he said as he hurried by.

Ben stared at him, confused, but the boy had already disappeared down the corridor. Was it his imagination, or were several students staring at him while giggling behind their hands? He felt his cheeks go hot and wondered whether there was breakfast cereal stuck to his face. He checked to make sure he hadn't put on his clothes back to front, but everything was in place. He shrugged and decided he was probably part of some practical joke, then picked up his backpack and entered the classroom.

Ms. Evans had already started class, so Ben slipped into his seat and hurriedly copied the instructions on the blackboard. He was late as well when the lunch-bell rang because he lost time separating his and Kimi's notes and assignments. He was still organizing papers when he reached the lunchroom, which was packed with noisy students.

He became aware of the stares by the time he was halfway across the hall. He slowed and saw students chatting behind their hands with their eyes glued on him. Some nudged each other and pointed.

A whole group of his classmates were gathered together, focused on something happening in their midst. When they saw him approach, he heard them whisper, "He's here!"

Some of them began to clap. Then, to his dismay, the cheering spread to the rest of the group, and all the way to the other tables. In no time, the lunchroom burst into clamour: there were whistles, exhilarated yells and hands slapping against the tables.

What the heck is going on?

From the center of the group, Wes and Tyler grinned happily.

Ben's face must have been livid because Tyler exclaimed, "Holy moly! Hang on a second! He hasn't seen it yet! Hey, Ben, come check this out!"

With dread in his heart, Ben made his way to the center of the group, where Tyler was sitting with an iPad in his hands, which he was holding up for all to see. He punched the screen and a YouTube page appeared. He selected a video and pressed the play button. The person who had filmed the video was not a professional because the image swayed from the sky to the white ground, then back and forth. Wes appeared briefly in the corner of the video, making everyone laugh.

The white background turned out to be a hill covered in snow, and when the camera peeked to the side of it, a frozen lake bordered by trees appeared. The camera stopped at the edge of the hill and focused on the boy and the dog standing before the lake, then on the girl who was ice-skating in the middle of it.

"It got twelve thousand views over the weekend, dude!" Tyler announced proudly. "It's gone viral! You're a star!"

Ben felt as if he had just been struck by lightning. He already knew what he was going to watch. There he was, trying to convince Kimi to get off the lake, then, just as he turned around to walk away, she fell through the ice and disappeared. There were gasps from his companions. Ben ran back and forth over the screen, then around the lake and across the ice to the place where Kimi had fallen. Soon he had removed his jacket and scarf, then plunged into the water. There was utter silence in the group as they waited for the protagonists to reappear.

By some incredible miracle, Mesmo was nowhere to be seen in the video, as he had been standing on the other side of the hill. Ben's head resurfaced a couple of times, though he was empty-handed, and there were murmurs of worry from his classmates. But when he broke the surface with Kimi in his arms, wild cheers and applause broke out around him.

The emotions that overwhelmed Ben while he watched the video were staggering. Crippling fear, anger and despair washed over him in multiple waves.

Twelve thousand people watched this video! Oh my God! Twelve thousand!

The adrenaline of the past days boiled over. Ben snatched at the iPad in Tyler's hands, inadvertently pushing against Wes who was sitting on a chair beside him. Wes shoved him back.

"Make it stop!" Ben shouted desperately, as the video continued to play.

By the time Ben had dragged Kimi out of the water and Maggie came running to their side, Ben's worst fear materialized as Mesmo appeared out of the corner of the screen. The alien turned his face briefly towards the camera, his distinct features appearing under his fur hat.

"Stop it!" Ben cried. He was so desperate he crushed Wes as he reached over him to grab the iPad.

"Hey!" Wes protested from his chair. He shoved at Ben who lost his balance and fell to the ground at the boy's feet, his back pushing the table aside.

Ben sprang up in a second. His mind burst with one thought: *Get the iPad!* As if that would stop the video from playing all over the world, from Timbuktu to the CSIS headquarters. This time he got ahold of the device, but Tyler had it in his grasp too tightly.

"What's the matter with you?" Tyler yelled at him angrily.

"I said shut it down!" Ben cried, pulling at the tablet. Both boys fell to the ground in a heap, pulling and shoving at each other. It didn't help when Wes joined the scuffle.

Like ants drawn to a piece of sugar, a chaotic circle of students formed around them, cheering as the fight unfolded.

Ben yelped when he received a punch in the eye. He must have kicked Tyler really hard because the boy groaned in pain. Boys and girls shouted them on excitedly.

Someone grabbed his arm and untangled him from the other two boys. He kicked and punched at the air, even though Joe, the school caretaker, had managed to get a hold of both Wes and Tyler. The circle widened as they were pulled apart.

Tears streamed down Ben's face. "You had no right!" he shouted furiously at Tyler.

✳ ✳ ✳

Ben sat in front of the Principal's office with an ice pack over his black eye–something he was thankful for because he could hide his feelings behind it. A sense of utter despair threatened to engulf him, making him want to weep his heart out. But he couldn't.

Opposite him, next to the office door, Wes and Tyler were glancing at him glumly. They had been told to sit quietly while Ms. Nguyen talked to their parents.

"Hey! Psst! Ben!" Tyler whispered.

Ben ignored him.

"Come on, man!" Tyler insisted. "We're sorry. We had no idea you'd feel like this. We thought you'd be proud of what you did! You're a hero, dude!"

Ben pressed the ice pack really hard, concentrating on the pain in his eye rather than the pain in his heart. How could Tyler ever begin to imagine what he was going through? His fear of Bordock and Inspector Hao, which he had managed to bottle up since his arrival in Canmore, cut through his body.

What if they saw the video?

The very thought paralyzed him.

Wes pressed a Kleenex against his bloody nose, and Tyler examined the big bump on his leg. Ben heard him note how 'cool' it was. The bruise was turning purple, green and yellowish.

Like my eye.

Wes bent over to whisper something to his friend, to which Tyler replied, "Yeah!" excitedly.

"Boys!" the assistant at the front desk warned.

The pair stiffened, suddenly taking a quiet interest in the carpet. Several minutes ticked by before Tyler ventured to catch Ben's attention again. "P-s-t! Hey, Ben! When this is over," he gestured to the Principal's office, "Let's do a revenge snowball fight."

Wes joined in excitedly. "Yeah, next Saturday, when Kimi's better. We can meet up at the Millennium Park."

Ben couldn't believe his ears. These boys, who were

in deep trouble, were already planning their next stunt. He wished he could have felt that laid back.

Tyler added, "We can sled there, too..." He was cut off when the door to the Principal's office opened and Wes and Tyler's parents emerged. Immediately, the two boys hung their heads in apparent shame.

Ms. Nguyen nodded Ben over, but just before he entered her office, he saw Tyler mouth *Millennium* at him.

As soon as the door closed, Ben fell into his mother's arms gratefully. He was intent on hiding behind his ice pack for the rest of the day and let her do the talking. But that didn't seem to be on the Principal's mind. The small woman played with her eyeglasses on the desk, staring at him intently. Ben ended up lowering the ice pack, wondering if she needed to see his two eyes before being able to speak.

A look of concern crossed her face when she saw the damage. "Ah, Ben!" she sighed. "What am I going to do with you?" She leaned back in her chair, her eyes boring into him. "I don't know whether to suspend you or give you a gold medal." She paused long enough for Ben to wonder what her verdict would be.

Her face broke into a smile. "Honestly? I think you're the bravest boy I've ever met in my entire career! You put another student's welfare before your own. You risked your life with no second thought as to the danger you were putting yourself in."

She turned her attention to Laura. "Ms. Anderson,

your son truly deserves the highest praise. I'm sure there must be some kind of Canmore medal for outstanding deeds to society. This could go much further than you could ever imagine..." She paused for effect, before finishing, "...but only if you want it to."

She was looking at Ben again. "Seeing that video and reliving that horrible experience must have been quite a shock for you, Ben. It's essential for you to understand that those boys had absolutely no right to be filming you or posting that video online for all to see, without your consent. That was a fundamental breach of privacy. And I want you to rest assured that the video was taken down immediately."

At her words, Ben breathed a little easier. He glanced at his mother, who squeezed his hand.

Ms. Nguyen proceeded very seriously. "Now this unusual event has sent shock-waves through the school and will continue to do so for some time. It is crucial for me to know your mind on this matter so that I can act appropriately. Would you like to share any thoughts, Ben?"

Ben crossed eyes with his mother, then said, "I just want this to go away. I want everything to go back to normal."

Laura added, "We're not looking for the limelight, Ms. Nguyen. We strongly insist on keeping our privacy intact and would appreciate any help you can give us."

The Principal nodded. "Yes, of course. You can count on my full support. In that case, if we are to avoid any interviews, filming, naming, handing out rewards, or such, I suggest you stay at home for the rest of the week, Ben. You are not grounded, but it's best you're not at school until I can calm the situation down. I will hold a staff meeting and instruct the teachers to talk to the students about the dangers of sharing private information on the internet. Goodness knows, we need that kind of debate in this day and age!"

Ben frowned. "But," he objected. "I have a civics exam on Friday."

Ms. Nguyen smiled. "Well, in that case, you can return on Friday if you feel up to it. I'll have Ms. Evans send you her notes and homework by e-mail this week so you can keep up. Does that sound fair?"

Ben nodded. He glanced at his mother, but he could not read her expression.

"The other question I must ask is something you need to weigh very carefully because it can affect the future of certain students." She crossed the fingers of her hands before her and said, "Will you be pressing any charges?"

Ben saw his mother straighten in her chair. "Charges?" she asked.

Ms. Nguyen pursed her lips. "Yes. Charges against Wes and Tyler for posting video material of Ben and Kimi without their consent. There's no need to answer right away, of course, but I'll need to know if you are going to want the police and lawyers involved."

Laura and Ben glanced at each other in alarm. "No,

no!" Laura said quickly. "Of course not! These boys were just fooling around. I'm sure their parents will talk some sense into them!"

Ben nodded vigorously in agreement.

Ms. Nguyen's relief was visible. "I'm glad you see it that way. I'm not defending their reckless actions, but, after all, they did call 911 without delay. At least it shows their hearts are still in the right place."

Ben echoed her words in surprise. "Wes and Tyler called the ambulance?"

Ms. Nguyen nodded. "Yes, Tyler sent Wes for help as soon as they saw Kimi fall through the ice. You can hear it in the video. Kimi was very lucky to be surrounded by so many good-willed people that day."

Ben sat back in his chair, fighting a grin. Those two boys would never cease to amaze him!

CHAPTER THIRTEEN

Breakthrough

By the time they got home it was late afternoon. Ben told Laura he wanted to rest, which suited her well because she needed to consult with Thomas about the day's developments.

Thomas arrived one hour later, followed by Mesmo not long after that.

"Sh!" Laura shushed the men when their voices rose at the news. "I don't want to wake Ben," she said.

Thomas pulled out a dining chair and sat heavily, while Laura finished filling Mesmo in. The television flickered with the volume down.

When Laura fell silent, Thomas said, "It's worse than you think. They knew about the ice incident at work."

"What?" Laura exclaimed. "But how?"

"It turns out some guy saw the ambulances at the lake and figured someone had fallen in. He started a thread on a Canmore community page on Facebook. I read it. No one has brought up Ben or Kimi's name yet, but it's only a matter of time."

Laura sagged into a sofa with her hand to her forehead. "Oh my gosh!" she breathed. "All this time we've been checking TV and radio stations..."

"...when we should have been checking social media." Thomas ended her phrase.

They stared at each other with a heavy silence.

"That's it, then. We have to leave," Laura stated finally.

"I've already looked into it," Thomas said. "But you can't leave. At least not right now. Two storm fronts are heading in from the plains. Once they hit the mountains, they will dump considerable amounts of snow on Canmore. The first one is due in a couple of hours. The second one on Friday night. We're stuck here for the first one, but I'm counting on getting you out before the second one hits, probably around noon on Friday."

Laura's brow creased. "That's a long time..."

Thomas interrupted. "You have no choice. Flying is out of the question right now. Driving would be insane. On the bright side, if we can't get out, no-one can get in either. So we shouldn't have any unwanted visitors until then."

Laura sucked in air, then nodded. "All right, Friday it is."

"NO!"

Laura's head snapped towards the stairs.

Ben was grasping the railing, his face flushed with anger. He yelled, "What about me? Is anyone interested to know what I want?" Without waiting for an answer, he stormed up the stairs and slammed his bedroom door.

Laura put a hand to her mouth. The adults fell silent. Mesmo made a gesture as if to follow Ben, but Laura stopped him. "No, it's ok. I'll go," she said, stepping forward.

But Mesmo was no longer looking at her. Instead, he stood frozen in front of the television. He pointed at the screen and gasped, "There!"

Laura was stricken. "What? Is it Ben?" She fully expected to see her son's face on the news. Instead, a reporter spoke in front of high windows behind which multiple large planes were stationed. The caption read: CANADIAN AIRLINE COMPANY IN JEOPARDY.

Thomas put up the volume.

"...the Alberta oil sands crisis has caught up with Canada's biggest airliner, Victory Air. Stocks have plummeted, and major investors have pulled out of the company. At this point, it would take a miracle to save the airliner," the reporter said.

Another reporter appeared on the screen. He was standing in front of a highrise surrounded by a flock of newspeople and cameramen. They followed a youngish man to the entrance of the building. The man pushed the cameras away with his hand in an attempt to get away from them. This time the caption read: VICTORY AIR HEADQUARTERS, TORONTO. The reporter spoke loudly into the microphone as he got shoved around by the crowd. "The spokesperson for the troubled airliner was not available for comments..."

"I don't understand," Thomas broke their concentration. "What are we looking at? That's Toronto, not Canmore."

"I saw him!" Mesmo exclaimed.

"Saw who?" Laura asked, confused.

Mesmo stared at her with wide eyes. "The man who is holding me!"

"Wha...?" She gaped at him in disbelief. "Thomas! Can you rewind that thing?"

"On it!" Thomas' thumb was already pressing the rewind button.

"There!" Mesmo said again.

Thomas pushed the play button. They stared at the stocky man with thick black and grey eyebrows and small green eyes behind black-rimmed glasses who appeared on the screen. His stance was relaxed and he smiled smugly as he shook hands with the President of the United States. The woman's voice reported over the images, "...just over a month ago, the CEO of Victory Air signed a billion dollar contract with the American government, leading economists to believe the airliner was in good shape. The CEO will release a statement later today..."

Laura gasped. "I know who that is!"

Thomas' head shot up. "You do?" he asked,

bewildered.

"Yes! And so do you. You may not have met him personally, but you will recognize his name."

Thomas frowned.

Laura sucked in air. "That's my father's neighbour, Victor Hayward."

✳ ✳ ✳

Laura knocked softly on Ben's door. She did not wait for him to answer but stepped into the bedroom, where she found him lying on his back, staring at the ceiling. When she sat on the edge of the bed, he turned to his side so she couldn't see his face. She rubbed his back, realizing he was crying.

After a long silence, Ben sobbed, "I don't want to leave."

"I know you don't," she said, staring at the floor. "I don't either."

Ben glanced at her with red eyes.

She gave him a sad smile. "This place has grown on us, hasn't it?"

Ben nodded, sniffling.

"Ben," she said more seriously. "We need to look at the bigger picture. We promised Mesmo we would help him. He's already saved us countless times." She leaned on the bed with her hands on either side of him so she could face him better. "We've had a breakthrough. I think I know where Mesmo is being held."

"Really?" Ben said, his eyes widening.

Laura nodded. "I want to stay here as much as you do, but as long as Bordock and the CSIS are looking for us, we'll never be safe. We have to free Mesmo so he can go home. Only then, will they leave us alone."

Ben's eyes lowered. After a pause, he said purposefully, "How do you know?"

She removed her hands and straightened, taken aback by his statement.

Ben insisted, "Seriously, Mom. How do you know for sure? I've been infected by alien blood. It's inside my body, spreading like a virus, turning me into some kind of freak. Mesmo can beam himself away to safety, but what about me? What about us?" He shook his head as if trying to rid his mind of the idea. "I don't want it. I don't want the skill, Mom. Mesmo can have it back." He rolled to his side again, his arms crossed over his chest.

Laura's shoulders sagged, Mesmo's words echoing in her mind. Bordock had forcefully taken a skill from Mesmo's wife. And she had died. Was Ben stuck with this skill indefinitely?

"Have you talked to Mesmo about this?" she asked, trying to sound in control.

His voice was muffled by a cushion. "Are you kidding? He wants me to have this skill. He's thrilled that I have it! He wants it to grow strong, so I can use it all the time."

Laura frowned. "Use it, for what?"

Ben faced her with angry eyes. "How should I know? Why don't you ask *him*?"

* * *

Laura shut the door to Ben's room quietly and leaned on the wall shakily. She placed her hands over her nose and mouth and closed her eyes tight.

She had gone to see Ben with the intention of reassuring him, but things hadn't gone as planned.

If they ever completed the daunting task of sending Mesmo home, would the police leave them alone? In her heart, she did not believe so.

And what was it about Ben's skill? Intuition told her Mesmo's interest in the skill went way beyond the fact that it had once belonged to his daughter. "I came to assess the planet." That's what he had said. But assess...for what?

Laura realized how little she knew about the alien whose destiny was intrinsically linked to theirs. Her father's letter warning her about Mesmo flashed before her eyes. *"He will crush you if he feels you are standing in his way."*

Her breath halted.

Would he really do that, if it came to it?

* * *

The stocky man's knuckles whitened as he grasped the side of the table, a large golden ring topping his ring finger. His nostrils flared and his small green eyes were hard. He looked like a bull seeing red.

Before him lay a computer screen from which a youngish man rubbed his pale face. Both men sat at desks though the first man had a view of a sprawling desert city while the other cowered in a dim room that resembled a hospital.

The youngish man blinked rapidly and wrung his hands together before him. "I'm sorry, Boss," he said meekly. "We can still contain this."

"*We?*" Victor Hayward seethed. He looked like he was about to explode. "Who do you think is going to an emergency meeting with the investors? I have the American military breathing down my neck. They are snapping at me like wild dogs." He leaned forward and said menacingly, "Maybe I should feed you to them instead."

The youngish man gulped visibly. Victor Hayward let him suffer for a bit, then said, "How did the media find out? Who told them the oil sands have dried up and we've been stalling to tell the world?"

"I...I don't know, Boss. We're still tracing the news. It obviously came from an investigative reporter..."

"...who slipped through the security *you* set up," Victor Hayward accused.

The man avoided eye contact. "Tell me what to do, Boss," he said, resigned. "I'll do it."

Victor Hayward leaned back into his tall office chair, letting air escape his nostrils as if he were letting off steam. "Sit tight," he said. "I need to get through this week, restore the investor's confidence, rub the media the right way, put on an angel face." He leaned forward again and jabbed a finger at the screen. "And then," he growled threateningly, "I'm coming home. And we are going to get down to business. Our martian friend's nursing days are over."

CHAPTER FOURTEEN

Rejection

Ben paced his room in frustration. He would honestly have preferred going to school rather than spend long days cooped up at home on his own. His mother had braved the wind and snow to walk to work that morning, while Thomas had had to wait for the roads to be decently cleared before he'd been able to make his way to Canmore Air. There were reports that schools and some businesses would close the next day if the snowstorm worsened. Laura had told Ben that Tim Hortons would remain open, however, due to the high demand for hot coffee, which suited her fine because she needed to work as many hours as possible before their departure.

Seeing as they planned on leaving that Friday at

noon, Ben begged his mother to let him take the civic's exam. Laura told him she did not like the idea, but he was adamant and refused to let go until she consented.

Now, alone at Thomas' house, Ben regretted having insisted so hard, because studying proved impossible. Strangely, it wasn't because their lives had been flipped upside-down, again. It was because, in the silence of the house, Tike was talking to him nonstop.

It started with a nudge in his mind, a playful thought, and before he knew it, Ben watched his hands begin to glow while he sat at his desk.

Tike let him know that he was thrilled to have made a connection again. He wagged his tail.

Wanna play?

Ben stiffened. He could feel a heart beating rapidly in excitement. Except it wasn't his heart. He glanced at Tike who rolled onto his back, paws in the air.

"Stop it!" Ben scolded, his own heart pumping a mixture of fear and blue venom. His ears rang with the blood flowing to his brain.

Play?

"No!" Ben yelled. He stuffed his notebooks in his backpack and raced down the stairs.

Tike followed more slowly, his ears and tail drooping.

What's the matter?

"Don't. Talk. To. Me!" Ben snapped, walking out with his boots and jacket unzipped.

A freezing wind slammed into him, sending snow

down his throat and neck. He shut the door on Tike and lumbered down the street, welcoming the biting cold.

What am I doing?

He couldn't believe what he had just done. He had shut the door on his best friend. Tears stung his eyes while he nervously tried to cover his bluish-lit hands with his gloves.

Tike was talking to him through the skill. But every time he did so, Ben knew that the skill was getting stronger, taking hold of him in ways he could not begin to comprehend. Every contact with Tike allowed the translation skill to infiltrate his core even more.

I'll never get rid of it!

He took a few steps through the snowstorm.

But this is Tike!

Why was he making such a big deal out of it? Wasn't talking to his own dog kind of awesome? Deep down, he agreed that it was, and part of him wanted to embrace the skill, yet at the same time, every fiber of his body continued to fight against it–because he feared it. What if human bodies weren't compatible with the alien element? What if the skill continued to make him sick until things became irreversible? What if the skill took over his thoughts? Or worse, what if it killed him? He was so involved in his own thoughts that he did not realize his feet were taking him to the Canmore General Hospital.

Kimi!

He felt a wave of comfort at the thought of seeing her. By the time he reached the hospital, the insides of his boots and the bottoms of his trousers were soaked.

When he found Kimi's room, she was resting against several piled-up cushions. Her long hair fell from both sides of her neck down to her arms. Her face was pale, and there were dark circles under her eyes, but her lips were rosy and she smiled.

"Ben!" She greeted him warmly. "What took you so long? I'm bored to death here!" she scolded, then blushed. "Sorry, bad choice of words."

Ben grinned, a fuzzy feeling replacing the cold he felt inside. "How are you?"

Her dark brown eyes twinkled. "They're pumping me with antibiotics. It seems to be working, though they insist I stay here for another couple of days." She rolled her eyes. "I don't know what I'm going to do with myself until then."

"Well, I know exactly what you're going to do," Ben said, dumping his backpack on a small table by the window. He pulled out his notes and handed them to her. "You're going to study for the civics exam."

"Are you kidding me?" she exclaimed, setting off in a fit of coughing.

Ben poured her some water and waited until she could breathe normally again.

"Sorry," she said with a feeble voice. "Happens sometimes."

"Don't talk," Ben ordered. "Just read."

He settled on a chair next to her, rested his chin on his arm with his notes before him on her bed. She eyed him for a few seconds as if trying to find something to scold him with, but in the end, she picked up the papers and began to read as well.

The minutes and hours ticked by as they studied quietly, absorbed by their task. For a brief moment at least, Ben forgot everything else, until a nurse came in and announced it was almost time for Kimi's dinner and medication.

Ben checked his watch, realizing how late it was. "Oops! Gotta go," he announced.

"Will you come back tomorrow?" Kimi asked with hopeful eyes.

"Of course! I look forward to another day of mutual boredom," Ben replied.

Kimi slapped him on the arm with her notes. They giggled, but that only set Kimi coughing again.

"Ok, ok, I'll behave," Ben said, having finished putting on his snow boots and jacket. "I'll see you tomorrow."

"Wait a minute," Kimi interjected, her face becoming serious. "Ben, Ms. Nguyen came and told me about the YouTube video." He stood by the door and saw her studying his face. "Are you all right?"

Ben shrugged, fighting a lump in his throat. "Sure. It's Wes and Tyler who should be worried. They got suspended for the rest of the week."

"Ben," she said again as if reluctant to let him go. "I... I haven't had a chance to thank you, you know, for what you did at the lake." She sucked in air and added, "You saved my life."

Ben stared at his feet, then shrugged again. "I'm just glad you're ok." Their eyes met for a moment.

"Excuse me," a woman said behind Ben. "Visiting hours are over. It's time for dinner."

"Oh, sorry," Ben apologized, stepping back as the nurse pushed in a trolley. The woman busied herself by Kimi's bed, placing a tray before her and arranging her pillows so she could sit up. Kimi pinched her nose and stuck out her tongue at the food tray.

Ben grinned and waved goodbye.

When he stepped into the street, it was already dark, and heavy snow whirled around him. He zipped up his jacket, covered his head with his hood, and stuffed his hands in his pockets.

"Can I join you?" Mesmo said, coming up beside him.

Ben shrugged and kept walking, though he had to admit having the alien beside him was extremely practical because the snow stopped slapping him in the face.

"How's Kimi?" Mesmo asked.

"Fine," Ben replied briefly as he struggled with his mixed feelings.

Why is it I always feel relieved when Mesmo is around?

"Do you want to talk about it?" Mesmo asked.

"Talk about what?" Ben retorted. He stopped to face the tall man. "You know what I want to talk about? I want to talk about the skill. You see, I don't want it. I want to be normal again. I want to be me. So I've decided I want you to take it back!"

Mesmo frowned. "We did talk about that. I told you it is yours now. It is a valuable gift..."

"It's not a gift!" Ben almost yelled. Pedestrians turned to look at them, so he lowered his voice. "It's not a gift. You can refuse a gift. But this one was imposed on me. I had no choice."

They walked on in silence, then Mesmo said, "I don't know why you struggle with it. All you have to do is learn to control it. I could teach you..."

"Stop!" Ben snapped. "Just...stop." He stepped away from the protective bubble into the swirling snow, leaving Mesmo staring at him.

With a few strides, the alien man caught up with him again. "Why do you fear it so?" he asked.

"*Why?*" Ben exclaimed, waving his gloved hands at him. "Jeez, do I have to spell it out to you? Maybe its because my hands are glowing? Maybe it's because I'm slowly losing control of my own thoughts? Or maybe because it's turning me into a freak, that's why!"

Mesmo was still frowning. "But why would it turn you into a freak? It is no different than a human skill."

"What are you talking about? Humans don't have skills like you!"

"Of course they do!" Mesmo replied. "I have met people with the skill of music, the skill of dancing, the skill of arts, the skill of invention..."

"The skill of *what?*"

Mesmo searched for the right words. "Take this snow for example. My skill is water: I simply manipulate the snow so it will not fall on us. Humans do not have this skill, so they perfected a different one: the skill of invention. They invented a device to cover themselves so they would not get wet."

Ben gaped. "An umbrella...? You're comparing your skill to...an umbrella?" He scoffed and shook his head.

Mesmo shrugged. "It may seem like nothing to you, but I find human creativity quite original." He fell silent suddenly as if a separate conversation had begun in his head.

They walked on, both lost in their own thoughts.

Even though Mesmo had shone a new light on the problem, Ben was still far from happy.

He's trying to convince me.

Ben spent the next day studying with Kimi. They tested each other and cleared up any remaining questions they had. Ben had snuck in a couple of doughnuts, which they munched on contentedly while they took a break. Ben lay at the end of the bed, staring at the ceiling.

"You know, I was thinking," Kimi began.

Ben groaned. "Please don't think. My brain is fried enough as it is."

Kimi kicked him with her foot from under the bedsheets.

"Shut up!" she scolded. "I'm serious. I was thinking about the lake."

"Oh," Ben's face darkened.

"No, listen. I was thinking about what I told you, about me not liking being First Nation and all. You were right, I wasn't thinking straight. I didn't mean what I said."

Ben straightened. "That's ok. You were angry. You had every right to be."

Kimi's eyes moved away from him. "No, it's more than that," she said. "You know, I really thought I was done for when I sank to the bottom of the lake. And the only thing I could think of was how stupid I was for hating myself." Her eyes fell on him again, twinkling from some inner fire. "You see, I realized that the problem isn't me being First Nation—the problem is my dad! I can't change what he thinks about my mom or me. But I can change how I think about myself. I don't have to look at myself through my dad's eyes. I have my own eyes to do that."

Her words resounded with certainty. "I am unique: I was born of two cultures. The one doesn't overshadow the other. On the contrary, they complement each other and make each other stronger, through me. Being born with two cultures is a gift, not a burden. I can create a new way of seeing the world and combine the two to solve problems. That's actually pretty awesome!"

She wrung her hands together in excitement as if she couldn't wait to apply her new philosophy. "It's not my problem if my dad couldn't adapt. It's not my job to suffer for it! I don't have to carry his burden. I know that now." She trailed off, consumed by an energy that burned brighter with her every word.

Ben hadn't moved an inch as her vision seeped deep into his core. He knew her words meant something vital to him too, only, he wasn't sure if he was ready to accept their meaning. He got off the bed and began gathering his notes and books.

Kimi was still caught up in her revelation. "I'll have to take you back to the lake this summer," she chatted. "It's not that bad, you know? Plenty of kids go swimming there when the days get hotter. And there's an ice cream truck that sells the best bubblegum flavour in the world. You'll see."

Ben had his back to her; he took his time filling up his backpack as he couldn't bear to face her.

I won't be here.

"Cool," he managed to utter.

"Ben?"

"What?" he tried to make his voice sound as normal as possible. He stuck his nose into his backpack as if he were searching for something.

"What's wrong?" Her question startled him.

"Huh?"

"You've been acting weird all week. Like you're trying to be cheerful for my sake, but you're just pretending. Something's wrong. I can tell."

How can she see right through me?

If he turned to face her, he would fall apart. He would have to tell her everything, and that would be the end of their friendship because she would never trust him again. His eyes welled with tears.

"Kimimela," Maggie's voice filled the room.

"*Iná*!" Kimi said cheerfully.

Ben watched them hug out of the corner of his eyes. He wiped his tears away swiftly.

"Ben," Maggie said, heading to him with her arms wide.

He had no choice but to turn this time. He was struck by how different Maggie looked. Her hair was neatly tied in a ponytail that went down to her waist. Her smile took years off her face, and she could almost have been mistaken for Kimi's older sister.

He fell into her arms gratefully because it allowed him to sob freely. She stroked his head for a long time. Finally, she took his head into both of her hands and placed her forehead on to his. "I thank you, *hokshila*[3]. You saved my butterfly and I am forever in your debt." She lowered her voice and added, "I don't know what it is your father did, but my people tell me he is a great spirit. Even a Wise One from the North has travelled to speak with him. Somehow I believe I am indebted to him, too."

They were still standing in this strange embrace when Laura and Thomas arrived.

"Hi," Laura said, casting a worried look in her son's

[3] *Hokshila* = child in 'Dakhona'.

direction. "We were looking everywhere for you, Ben."

Maggie patted Ben on the shoulder and took out a tissue to wipe her eyes. She hugged Laura and Thomas, then went to sit by Kimi's bed. "I am glad you are all here," she said. "I have something to tell you." She took Kimi's hand and continued, "Some years ago, I lost my husband. He abandoned Kimi and me. For a long time, I suffered from this. I blamed myself for it, told myself I could have done more. I turned away from my identity, from my people, and I turned away from my daughter. I became a shadow of myself." She paused, struggling with her words. "I turned away from everything that most mattered to me, and instead, sought refuge in a poison, which I used to drown my grief." She gazed straight at Kimi and said, full of emotion, "I became an alcoholic."

Ben felt a shift in the room at the meaningful confession.

Maggie squeezed her daughter's hand and claimed, "I am Magaskawee. I am of the Dakhona people. You are my daughter, Kimimela, and I will heal now, for you."

Kimi's face crumbled as she threw herself into her mother's arms. There wasn't a dry eye in the room. When Maggie pulled away from her daughter, she stared at the floor and admitted, "The road will be hard, Kimimela. I will need your help."

Kimi nodded, her face puffy with emotion.

Thomas cleared his throat and went to stand before Maggie. "I would like to help," he said shakily. "That is, if you would let me..."

Maggie frowned as she stood up. "Why?"

Thomas took both of her hands in his and looked deep into her eyes. "I think you know why," he said softly.

"Ben," Laura whispered as she pulled him by the arm. She nudged her head towards the door. "Time to go."

They slipped out of the room. Just before the door closed, Ben saw Kimi glance at him with a huge smile and eyes that sparkled in amazement.

Ben stared at his mother as they walked to the elevator. "Thomas? And Maggie?" he exclaimed, his eyes wide.

Laura only smiled.

Ben jumped in front of her, walking backwards to stay ahead. "Thomas?" he repeated. "And Maggie?"

Laura's smile widened.

Ben's surprise turned into a grin, and he nodded in approval.

"Cool!"

CHAPTER FIFTEEN

Not Human

When Kimi entered the classroom on Friday morning, the students broke into loud cheers of welcome. Wes and Tyler, who had been allowed back for the civics exam, hooted the loudest.

Kimi blushed and hid her smile behind her books. Her hair tumbled over her loose turtleneck sweater. The burgundy colour went well with her dark eyes and Ben thought she was easily the prettiest girl in class.

She winked at him as she settled at her desk.

"It's good to have you back, Kimi," Ms. Evans said warmly.

Kimi responded with a raucous cough, but she gave a thumbs up and nodded.

Ms. Evans exclaimed. "Oh dear! All right, good thing

it's not an oral exam. Best to leave your voice alone today, I think."

She distributed the exam papers, checked her watch and indicated that they could start.

Ben turned over the papers and scanned through the questions. He glanced at Kimi, and they exchanged a grin; they knew the answers.

This is going to be easy.

Ben pushed the idea that he was flying out of Canmore forever that day to the back of his mind, and began scribbling. Thirty minutes into the hour, he paused to stretch his back. He checked on his classmates. They were hunched over their desks in concentration—even Wes and Tyler, he noted. He rubbed his neck, then leaned over to continue writing.

His hands were glowing. He jumped, his heart racing. He glanced around hurriedly to make sure no-one had noticed, then froze at the sight outside the window.

On the windowsills, a dozen crows sat with their beady eyes aimed at him. One of them cawed, while the others resembled silent, unmoving gargoyles from a gloomy cathedral.

He tried to ignore the familiar sensation of blood rushing to his ears, but there were too many crows, and their chatter seeped into his mind. The exam answers he had formulated evaporated as if blown away by a cumbersome wind. The birds were trying to tell him something, he knew, but he wasn't willing to hear. A cold sweat broke above his brow as he tried to block off the intrusion into his mind.

I won't listen!

He hung his head a few inches from the papers on his desk so he wouldn't have to acknowledge that contact had been made, but all he saw were blurry words under the tip of his pen. The roaring in his mind became stronger, and part of him knew the message was urgent, that he should listen.

A loud knock startled him back into awareness of the classroom. The Principal entered with a distinctly troubled look on her face. "I'm sorry to interrupt the class, Ms. Evans. I know you're in the middle of an exam, but could I borrow Ben for a minute?" She was clearly unhappy. Her eyes and those of the rest of the class turned to Ben.

Something furry scuttered between Mrs. Nguyen's legs. Tike dashed across the classroom. At seeing him, Ben's mind exploded with an imminent threat.

Run!

Not a doubt was left in Ben's mind. He knew then precisely what Tike was trying to tell him. Panic surged through his body. He jumped to his feet, his chair falling over in his haste. At the same time, Hao and Connelly entered the classroom, shoving Mrs. Nguyen aside.

Ben's eyes searched wildly for an exit, but the only way out was barred by the agents. Like an animal caught in a trap, he staggered back into the wall.

An electric silence fell over the classroom.

Hao took a careful step forward. He was aware of

the twenty-four pairs of eyes that were on him, because he forced a smile, "Hello, Benjamin. Would you step outside, please?"

Ben shook his head wordlessly.

Hao raised an eyebrow. His hands twitched by his side. He gestured meaningfully towards the students. "Come now, there's no need to make a scene. Don't make this harder on yourself."

Ben felt his resilience fading like snow in the desert sun, yet he could not make himself cross the only space of freedom that remained between him and the agent. The cold eyes that Connelly aimed at him from behind Hao glued him to the ground.

There's no way I'm going with him!

Hao's irritation was palpable. He did not need to raise his voice, because his sharp tone was unmistakeably demanding. "Benjamin Archer, you are under arrest. You will step out of this classroom at once!"

The Inspector's words triggered a hidden source of anger within Ben. How dare this man threaten him? How dare he remove him from the safety of his classroom and uproot his life at the snap of his fingers?

"No!" he said, the word born deep within. He wasn't sure what he was doing—he was driven by instinct rather than common sense, but he didn't care. This situation was wrong and he meant to let everyone know it was so.

I'm not going down without a fight!

"No!" he said again, this time with more vigour. "I'm not going with you! I've done nothing wrong and you know it! I'm innocent until proven guilty. I deserve to be treated like a human being!"

"You are NOT a human being!" Hao's words flew across the room and planted themselves like knives into Ben's heart. He swayed at their power.

A deathly silence that would rival the eye of a hurricane filled the room. A pencil rolled slowly off a desk, then clattered loudly to the ground.

Hao blinked and glanced at the multitude of wide eyes that were on him. He sucked in air as he straightened. "Enough," he scowled, gesturing to Connelly. "I don't have time for this. Get him."

The alien who used Connelly's traits as a disguise, strode purposefully towards Ben and Ben cowered at his every step. Then, suddenly, the Shapeshifter stopped and stared down in confusion.

"No, you're not," Tyler announced, planting himself in front of Connelly. Ben's classmate inflated his chest and crossed his arms. "Ben's my friend and I won't let you take him."

"Tyler!" Ben whispered urgently. He could see the muscles in Connelly's neck tighten.

"Me, neither," a voice said, and in an instant, Wes was rubbing shoulders with Tyler.

Voices flared, chairs scraped on the floor and students flocked to Wes and Tyler's side.

"Now wait a minute..." Ms. Evans had sprung out of her chair, arguing with Hao.

Ben could not escape the Shapeshifter's glare. He

could sense the tenseness in the bald man's face as more and more students rushed to stand between them.

"Don't!" Ben said weakly, praying that the alien would not burst like a nuclear warhead, but his warning was lost in the raucous objections.

A gust of freezing wind hit him in the neck. A hand pulled him aside.

"This way!" Kimi urged.

Ben blinked.

Kimi had opened a classroom window and was already halfway through it. Catching on, Ben picked up Tike and shoved the dog after her. Kimi slid down a ledge and jumped into the packed snow not far below. Ben stuck out his own head and caught his breath: there were hundreds—no, thousands—of crows littering the trees, school rooftop, windowsills and sky all around him.

No sooner had he slipped onto the ledge, than a multitude of wings unfolded around him. A deafening noise of grating caws and clicks filled the air. Ben felt a whoosh of feathers as the birds dove inches from his head, then shot through the open window behind him, triggering shrieks from terrified students caught inside the classroom.

Ben's brain exploded with noise, not so much from the thunderous cawing outside, but from the staggering clamour inside his brain.

Run! Danger! Get out! What are you waiting for? Get away!

Ben pressed his glowing hands over his ears and

screamed. His body weight dragged him over the edge and he landed in the snow with a thud. The crows were outside and inside of him. He was a boy lying in the snow, but he was also a thousand birds swirling through the air and diving into the hectic classroom.

"Ben!" Kimi's distressed call came through to him.

He gasped in pain and felt the cold snow beneath his body. It brought him back to his senses long enough to stand and stagger away from the school with Kimi's support.

When they were two blocks away, the sudden void in his mind made him retch horribly.

He knew that Kimi was watching his glowing hands with a mixture of fear and wonder. But she grabbed him under the arm and pulled him down the street. The cold seeped through their clothes and their shoes, as they hadn't been able to put on snow gear.

Ben was vaguely aware of his surroundings and of Kimi, who shot him anxious glances as they advanced. He felt utterly exposed to the skill. In his mind's eye, the blue filaments grew arms and attached themselves to millions of neurons in his head, weaving an intricate web through his brain, and he was too weak to fight it.

Tike entered his thoughts, sending him an image of police cars with swirling lights in front of a townhouse. Ben's stomach heaved.

"Wait!" he wheezed as he stopped Kimi from dragging him on. He took a deep breath to settle the nausea and tried to focus on his surroundings. "Not

Thomas' place," he said. "Too late. Police are already there."

Kimi gave him a strange look, but said, "Can you make it to my house?"

Ben nodded.

She took him by the arm again, but Ben gasped suddenly.

"What?" Her eyes widened as they stopped again.

"My mom!" Ben exclaimed. "She doesn't know! I have to warn her!"

"Come on!" Kimi urged. "I'm taking you home. Then, I'll get your mom." She pulled him forward through the snow-packed streets. Light snowflakes floated through the air.

They made it to Kimi's house. She opened the door and shoved him in. "I'll be right back," she said, heading away before he could say anything.

"Kimi, is that you?" Ben heard Maggie say. She appeared in the living room door and frowned worriedly. "Ben?" She took him by the shoulders and led him through the door, where he found Thomas sitting on a couch and placing a cup of coffee on a low table.

He took one look at Ben and sprang up. "What is it?" he asked hurriedly, catching Ben in his arms.

Ben choked up into his sweater. "They're here!"

✳ ✳ ✳

"Enjoy your latté," Laura said, as she handed a steaming cup to a customer over the counter. The customer was headed to the door of the coffee shop when it swung open and Laura saw someone collide head-on with him. The latté flew through the air, then landed in a splash on the floor. "Hey!" the customer yelled, but the offender did not offer an excuse and instead searched the place with frantic eyes.

"Kimi?" Laura exclaimed, recognizing the girl's long, black hair.

Kimi rushed around the counter and placed an icy hand on Laura's arm. She wanted to speak but instead broke down in a fit of coughs. "Girl, you're freezing!" Laura scolded worriedly. "Where's your jacket?"

Kimi caught her breath and stared straight at Laura. "Ben said to come quick!" she said, wheezing.

Laura felt her heart drop. "Where's Ben?" she asked urgently, already removing her Tim Horton's cap.

"My place," Kimi coughed.

"Come on." Laura led Kimi to the back of the coffee shop.

"Some men came to the school looking for him." Kimi explained.

"Hey, lady," the unfortunate customer called after them over the counter. "I want my latté!"

Laura dropped the cap next to a sink, grabbed her winter jacket and wrapped Kimi in it. "Let's go," she said, heading for the back exit.

"Hold up! Laura!" someone called behind them. A large woman with a similar cap hurried to catch up with them. "Where are you going?" the woman puffed. A pin attached to her apron said MANAGER.

Laura let go of Kimi. "I'm sorry, Rhina, I have to go," she said.

"But...are you coming back?" Rhina asked in dismay.

Laura shook her head. Her chin quivered.

Rhina's shoulders sagged, but she said, "Wait a minute. You can't go without your pay." She dug into her fanny pack around her waist and fished out a handful of dollar bills and coins. "Here, take it. Don't worry. I'll figure things out with the others later."

"No...I..." Laura objected, pushing the woman's hand away.

"Take it!" the woman insisted. "It's all I have on me. It's your share of this week's tips. You've earned it."

Laura hesitated, then accepted the money. "Thank you," she said, her eyes falling on the unhappy customer.

Rhina rolled her eyes. "Don't you worry about him, dear. We'll fix him up with a gift card or something."

Laura hugged her. "Goodbye," she said, holding back the tears.

"You take care, now, you hear?" the woman insisted.

Laura nodded, then headed through the exit with Kimi. A gentle snow fell around them as they hurried down the cold streets.

CHAPTER SIXTEEN

Dreamcatcher

Laura found Thomas and Maggie poring over a large map, which they had spread out on the countertop of the kitchen island.

"Where's Ben?" she asked as she rushed to join them.

"Outside," Thomas pointed to the outer deck which lay off the dining room.

Laura made as if to join him, but Thomas grabbed her firmly by the arm. "There's no time."

Laura set her jaw, then nodded in understanding. "What's the plan? Are we flying?" She stared at the map.

Thomas shook his head. "Too late for that. Canmore Air is swarming with cops."

Laura gaped. "What do we do?"

"Do about what?" Mesmo's voice startled them.

"Mesmo!" Laura felt a wave of relief.

"Who's Mesmo?" Maggie frowned.

Thomas and Laura stared from Mesmo to Maggie.

Thomas took Maggie's hand. "Maggie, this man is not Jack Anderson. His real name is Mesmo. I know this is a lot to ask, but I need you to trust him. I need you to trust me."

Maggie glanced thoughtfully at the tall man in the fur hat. "My people have told me that Angakkuq crossed the country to confer with a great spirit here. I don't know who...or what you are. I don't know what you did to my daughter. But I do know she is alive, thanks to you." Her eyes fell on Thomas. "Tell me what you need."

Thomas' brow relaxed and he nodded in thanks. "It's not Mesmo I'm worried about. We need to find a safe passage out of Canmore for Ben and Laura. Mesmo will follow them in his own manner." He turned his attention to the map. "There aren't many options. We obviously can't send them back west. They need to go east." He followed Highway 1 with the tip of his finger until it reached the city of Calgary. He jabbed at the name on the map. "There!"

"But how?" Laura studied the area around Thomas' finger. "The only way out of Canmore is north, by way of this road that links to the highway. They'll have set up barricades and will be checking every single car driving out of Canmore."

They stared at the map as if waiting for it to give them an alternative.

Suddenly, Maggie said, "The Kananaskis!" She bent over the map and pointed at the main road linking Canmore to the highway. "Look," she said. "Before you reach the highway, you turn left into this small road. It makes a U-turn and will take you south, past Canmore. You follow it all the way down to...here." She indicated a spot that seemed lost in the middle of nowhere. "There is a crossing here that will take you over the Kananaskis Mountain Range."

"That's a huge detour!" Thomas exclaimed.

"It is," Maggie agreed. "But once they reach the other side of the mountain, they can travel north again and rejoin the highway between Canmore and Calgary—here."

Laura contemplated the map. She followed Maggie's instructions in her mind and realized they would basically be making a huge circle around Canmore that would eventually get them back to the highway.

"I don't know," Thomas' voice reflected his uncertainty. "A snowstorm is approaching. I think it's too risky."

"They can make it," Maggie insisted. "If they leave now, they should be over the Kananaskis in a couple of hours, before the worst of the storm hits."

Thomas glanced at Laura. "What do you think? You're the one who has to drive."

Laura straightened, suddenly realizing that she and Ben would be on their own soon. "What about you?" she asked.

Thomas pressed his lips together, his eyes on Maggie. "I think I'm going to stay this time."

Maggie offered him a smile.

Thomas spoke to Laura, his eyes still on Maggie, "I don't think the secret services will be very interested in me anymore." He fished keys out of his pocket and gave them to Laura. "Here, you can have my car."

"No," Maggie objected. "They'll be looking for it. Take mine. It's a pickup truck with sturdy wheels. It will get you over the mountains."

"Thank you," Laura whispered, her head swirling at the task ahead.

✳ ✳ ✳

Ben stared at nothing in particular. He sat outside on the top steps of a wooden stairway that joined the deck with the yard. He had grabbed one of Kimi's jackets, covered his head with the cape and leaned against the wooden railing.

Mesmo appeared in his field of vision and crouched beside him.

Ben hid his face under the cape unable to face the alien. The boy's words came out with difficulty, his voice empty of emotion. "Hao said I'm not human." His chin began to tremble. "I don't know what I am anymore." He finally turned and glared at the alien. "This is all your fault," he said accusingly, his nostrils flaring.

"Benjamin..." Mesmo began.

"Leave me alone." Ben lowered his face into the cape again. His tone was final. He felt Mesmo pause, then move away. He wanted the alien to stay and comfort him, but the part of him that was angry and unaccepting wouldn't allow it. He heard the deck door slide open and for a moment his mind tricked him into believing the alien had doubled back.

Mesmo can't open doors, he reminded himself.

Black army boots came to stand beside him. "My mom said to try these on," Kimi dangled snow boots at him. "She said you're going over the mountain in our pick-up truck. She's putting together some backpacks with emergency gear. Every Dakhona knows to never approach the Kananaskis without emergency gear, even if you're in a pick-up truck. The mountains can be unforgiving. The Dakhona regard them with the greatest respect."

Since he didn't react, she plopped beside him with a sigh, dumping the snow boots before her as if they weighed a ton. They didn't speak for a painfully long time.

Ben heard Kimi's voice waver when she broke the silence. "You knew this was coming, didn't you?" she asked. "Back at the hospital, you already knew you were going to leave..." Her tone wasn't accusing, but it hurt anyway.

He looked at her without answering. He found tears streaming down her cheeks and his heart tightened. "I don't have a choice." He wrung his hands together. "I have to go."

"But, it's your dad they're after, isn't it? Maybe you could stay, and your dad could go away for awhile..." He heard the false hope in her voice.

Ben shook his head. "He's not my dad."

She knit her brows.

Ben sighed. "My dad died shortly after I was born. I never got to know him." He gestured vaguely inside the house. "His name is Mesmo. And, no, I can't stay. He goes wherever I go. We're stuck together in that way."

She blinked and turned away. After a silence, he heard her say with a touch of unease, "Ben? What did that man mean, when he said you're not...human?"

It hurt to hear her say it just as much as when Hao had said it.

Ben shuffled his feet in the snow, then breathed, "It's true." He listened to his own words, trying to accept them.

She turned to him abruptly, her eyes filled with tears. "No, it's not!" she said vehemently. "Don't be daft! You're my favourite human being in the whole world." She wrapped her arms around him and cried into his shoulder.

The sweet gesture cracked his resolve. Overcome with emotion, Ben shut his eyes and squeezed her tightly.

They were still hugging when Laura stepped onto the deck, her arms full of bulging backpacks. "Ben?" Her voice broke up their embrace.

Kimi stared at Ben with reddened eyes. She leaned over to him and pecked him with cool, soft lips on the corner of his mouth, then ran into the house.

Ben watched her disappear, his heart breaking slowly.

"Ben?" His mother's voice called softly. "We have to go."

He nodded forlornly, then changed into the snow boots. When he stood up, he began to remove Kimi's knee-length jacket from his shoulders, but Maggie stopped him. "No, keep it. You'll be needing it."

He nodded in thanks, then accepted one of the backpacks that Laura handed to him. They hugged Maggie and Thomas, then got into the pick-up truck, which was parked next to the veterinary building. Laura took the wheel of the four-door pick-up truck while Mesmo sat on the passenger side. Ben slipped into the back. Tike jumped on his lap.

"We'll get the truck back to you somehow," Laura reassured Maggie.

"Just be safe," Maggie replied, squeezing Laura's hand through the window.

The screen door slid open and Kimi came running up to them. Ben rolled down his window as she approached. She reached out and placed something in his hand. It was a flat, circular object, the size of his palm, with a finely woven net inside. Some beads and feathers hung below it.

"What is it?" Ben asked in wonder.

"It's a dreamcatcher," she explained. "I made it with my grandmother on the reservation. It will protect you from bad spirits."

Ben felt a wave of gratitude. "It's beautiful. Thanks!" He stared at the carefully knotted strings that resembled a spider's web. "But, I don't have anything for you!"

She placed her hand on her heart as she stepped away from the truck. "You gave me back my family." She smiled as she joined Maggie and Thomas.

Laura revved up the pick-up, and soon their friends disappeared behind the veterinary clinic. She headed down the main street of Canmore as snow began to fall more insistently.

"Mom!" Ben shouted suddenly, making her hit the breaks with force. Ben and Tike slipped forward into the back of Laura's seat.

"What?" she said in alarm.

Ben rubbed his nose.

"Put on your seat belt!" she scolded.

He did so in a hurry. "Your asthma inhaler!" he said. "Do you have one?"

He saw her eyebrows draw together. She drove slowly for a while as if in deep thought. "No, I don't have one. Truth is, I haven't used one in months." She glanced at Mesmo curiously.

"Like me!" Ben gasped. "I haven't had a panic attack either."

They both stared at Mesmo as if expecting the alien to explain the mysterious disappearance of their symptoms, but Mesmo pointed ahead. "We are nearing the highway ramp," he said.

Ben stretched his neck. In the flurry of snow, he spotted the whirling lights of a dozen police cars in the distance.

"Where's that other exit Maggie was talking about?" Laura's anxiousness was palpable. "Ben, check the map, would you?" She shoved the map to the back and he scrambled to open it wide enough to find their location.

If only we could use Google Maps like every normal person!

The vehicle slowed but inevitably neared the ramp. A line of cars was being monitored one at a time before being released to the highway.

Laura came to a stop. "Ben!" she urged.

"Uh..." Ben scrunched at the map in his haste. "Turn back, Mom! We missed it. Turn back!"

The tires screeched on the snow as she made a full u-turn. They squinted at the scattered houses and snow-covered trees.

"Got it!" Laura exclaimed, swinging the pick-up to the right into a small street they had previously missed.

Ben glanced through the rear window, and his heart leapt into his throat. A couple of police cars had detached themselves from the main body of vehicles at the ramp. "They're coming!"

CHAPTER SEVENTEEN

Trapped

Laura grasped the wheel, the knuckles of her hands turning white from the pressure. The windshield wipers worked wildly to keep the snow out of her vision, but even so, it was becoming harder to distinguish anything on the gloomy road bordered by dense forest. There wasn't a soul in sight, so she switched on the headlights and pressed on the pedal to pick up speed. The motor sent a satisfying lurch of power into the tires.

"I thought the storm wasn't due until later," Ben echoed her thoughts. She bit her lip and tried to ignore a nagging feeling in the pit of her stomach. The flashing red-and-white lights pressed her on. There was no turning back now.

The pick-up truck wound its way through the

lonesome road bordering the towering Kananaskis Mountain Range. Laura's brow beaded with sweat as she checked the rearview mirror, but she didn't think the police were making any headway on them.

"Watch it, Mom!" Ben warned. "We should be nearing the crossroad going over the mountain."

Laura slowed down reluctantly. They couldn't afford to miss the exit this time. After a couple of minutes, Mesmo's sharp eyes found it. "There it is!" He pointed.

Laura hit the breaks. She switched off the headlights and swerved to the left into an almost invisible crossroad that immediately began to ascend.

"Stop!" Mesmo ordered. "Let me out of the truck."

Laura obeyed without a second of hesitation.

She watched through the rear-view mirror as the alien ran to the back of the truck and placed his hands on the tracks that the tires had imprinted into the snow. A wave of blue light flowed from his fingers to the bottom of the road, melting the snow until it looked smooth and even.

He hurried back and said, "That should keep them off for a while."

Laura realized he must have turned the snow into a sheet of ice behind them. She revved up the engine again and began the steep climb into the evening sky.

✳ ✳ ✳

Hao placed his hand on the dashboard as if that would make the Sheriff's car go faster. He leaned in, trying to make out the pick-up truck in the dark tunnel of trees ahead.

"Don't lose them!" he urged the Sheriff who was at the wheel.

After several minutes of tense silence, the police radio crackled. The Sheriff answered, never taking his eyes off the road.

Hao glanced at him questioningly.

"It's Connelly," the Sheriff said. "He says we need to turn back. He thinks they're heading into the Kananaskis."

"The what?" Hao's face went red.

The Sheriff pointed at the looming peaks alongside the road. "The Kananaskis Mountain Range."

Hao swore as he whirled to check behind them. Two police cars were still following them, but a couple of others had stopped some way back. "What does he think he's doing? Tell him to get over here! That's an order!"

The Sheriff spoke into the radio, then glanced at Hao. "One of the cars got stuck at the crossroad. They're on a patch of black ice. But Connelly says he can get through. He's convinced the fugitives are on their way up."

"Black ice?" Something triggered in Hao's mind. He remembered the unnatural formation of ice at the Vancouver Police Department.

He squinted ahead. Earlier, he'd been able to follow the pick-up truck in the distance; now there was only darkness and swirling snow.

"All right! Back up, back up!"

The Sheriff did so, but he warned, "The storm is picking up strength. It's going to be hell up there. I may have to pull off the search."

"You're not pulling anything off, Sheriff!" Hao flared. "Or shall I have you reflect on that with the High Inspector?"

The Sheriff straightened his cap and pursed his lips, but made no comment as he drove carefully along the edge of the crossroad to avoid the slippery patch in the middle. An officer tried to manoeuvre his car off the ice patch. A second police car stopped next to it to help.

The Sheriff pointed his Toyota back to the middle of the road, which wound steeply between the fir trees. Hao bent forward, taking in the massive form of the Kananaskis Mountain Range that reached for the sky like jagged knives, attracting black storm clouds to their peaks.

"You've got to be kidding me!" he breathed.

✳ ✳ ✳

A heavy silence hung in the pick-up. Laura had switched on the headlights again, but even so, she had a hard time making out the road before her. Large snowflakes hit the windshield. No sooner were they shoved aside by the wipers, than a dozen even bigger flakes replaced them.

"They weren't fooled," Ben said. "They're still after us. I think I saw the headlights."

Laura tensed as she pressed on the speed pedal, excruciatingly aware that she was going too fast. The truck's nose pointed upward as she weaved her way further and further up the mountain. The motor strained on the unfriendly path. After hairraising minutes, the pick-up began to level out again, indicating they were reaching the summit, which was squeezed between even higher black mountain peaks. Breathing a bit easier, she glanced at Mesmo, who was focused on the road ahead. "You don't have to be here, you know?" she told him.

He met her eyes and his voice was firm. "I do."

Laura bit her inner lip, relieved that he wasn't abandoning them.

The pick-up skidded. Laura steered the wheel sharply to the right, but lost control of the vehicle. It slid for a heart-stopping moment. There was a crunching sound and the truck jolted to a stop.

"What is it?" Ben asked fearfully.

Laura tried to reverse. The tires screeched in protest. "We're stuck!" She opened the car door, inviting a biting cold inside. She stepped out and Mesmo came around to stand by her side. The front tire was buried in deep snow.

"Mom! They're catching up!" Ben rushed up behind them.

Laura could hear the wailing police sirens

approaching too fast for comfort. She whirled to face Mesmo. "Get us out of here! Release the tires!"

"There's no time!" he yelled through the storm. "I sense Bordock nearby. The mountain is our best bet. Follow me!" He turned and stepped headfirst into the darkness away from the road.

"*What?*" Laura's voice rose in panic. "Are you crazy?"

"Mom, hurry!" Ben followed Mesmo.

"Ben!" Laura cried as he disappeared into the flurry of snowflakes. "Come back! It's too dangerous! Ben!"

She rushed into the deep snow after him, her breath coming in quick gasps. She hesitated, then backtracked and snatched one of the backpacks from the truck. She wanted to get the other one, but the police cars burst into view behind her. Laura dove after her son just as the first police car slid off the road and collided headlong with the pick-up. The others screeched to a stop just in time.

"Mom!" She heard Ben's muffled shout in the swirling snow before her. Behind her, the lights of the police cars offered the only island of safety on the massive mountain.

"Laura Archer!" A man moved in front of the headlights of one of the police cars. She recognized Inspector Hao's voice. "Don't be foolish. You're heading to your death."

Laura walked away from him, though at a slower pace. Her heart beat as fast as a hare's as she realized he was telling the truth.

"Laura Archer! Think of your son's safety!"

She sobbed and tripped into the snow. "Ben!" she shouted, searching the darkness.

"Over here!" His voice sounded far away.

Laura stood again and walked blindly into the storm.

"Let's go!" Hao pressed his hand on the gun at his side as he made to follow Laura.

The Sheriff grabbed him by the arm. "That's out of the question. Those fugitives have sealed their fate. But that doesn't mean I'm going to risk my men's lives as well." He shot a glance at Hao. "I'll let you reflect on that with your High Inspector." The Sheriff didn't wait for Hao to answer and gestured at his other men to get back in their cars. One of them panted up the road towards them. "I can't find him!"

"Find who?" The Sheriff asked hurriedly.

The officer pointed at Hao. "His colleague. I saw him run to the pick-up when we arrived, but now he's not there anymore."

Hao felt his blood boil all the way to his face. He turned to the darkness and bellowed. "C-O-N-N-E-L-L-Y!"

* * *

"Mesmo! Wait up!" Ben shouted as the alien strode effortlessly in the snow. Ben stumbled after him to try and stay in the protective bubble the alien was emitting around him to keep the snowstorm at bay. "Not so fast! I can't see Mom."

They stopped and searched the way they had come. Ben tucked a shivering Tike inside his jacket.

They saw powerful searchlights on top of the police cars sweeping the area, but they did not quite reach far enough to catch the fugitives.

"Where is she? She was right behind us," Ben said worriedly. Then, the light briefly caught Laura's shape as she stumbled on with a large backpack. She was heading away from them.

"Where is she going?" Ben frowned, then his voice stuck in his throat as a dark shape loomed before her in the passing searchlight.

✳ ✳ ✳

"Ben? Where are you?" Laura shouted as she raised her arm to protect her eyes from the swirling snowflakes.

"Over here!" Ben said right before her.

She let out a breath of relief and stepped forward, only to stagger headfirst into a bald man.

She opened her mouth to scream, but he clamped a

steel hand over her mouth and pulled her down in the snow, just as a beam of light swept over them.

"Hi, *Mommy*," Connelly sneered with Ben's voice. She saw Connelly's eyes switch from green to honey-brown.

She struggled to escape from his grip, but instead, she felt something cold clasp onto her wrist, and before she knew it, they were connected to each other with handcuffs.

Hao shouted from the road, "Connelly! Get back here!" Several flashlights pierced the flurry of falling snow as the officers called for the missing agent.

"Let's go!" Connelly growled, picking up Laura's backpack and heaving it onto his shoulder. The Shapeshifter pulled at the cuffs, making Laura lurch after him.

"No, wait!" she yelled, but he held her with an iron grasp, pulling her further away from the road. "Ben!" she gasped. "You can't leave him! He has no protection! He won't survive on his own!" She turned her head and shouted, "Ben!"

"Good idea," Connelly jeered. "Call him. Let's have him join our little party."

Laura's eyes widened and she fell silent instantly.

Catching her look of fear, Connelly chuckled, sending a chill up-and-down her spine.

✳ ✳ ✳

"Mom!" Ben shouted, panic surging through his body when he realized what was happening. He dropped Tike and heaved himself up a snowy ledge to rush to his mother's aid. Instead, his feet slipped beneath him, and he skidded several feet down on his back. Tike bumped into his head as he collided with a tree. He blinked the stars from his eyes and got up immediately, then realized that Mesmo was a little way up with his hands placed in the snow. He had turned the slope into ice.

"What are you doing?" Ben yelled furiously, trying to get up but sliding back every time. "Bordock's got my mom! We have to save her!"

Mesmo reached him with a couple of strides and stared at him intensely. "No! That's exactly what Bordock wants. If you go after him, that will be the end of us."

"But my mom!" Ben shook all over.

"Calm down!" Mesmo urged.

"*Calm down?*" Ben howled. He threw himself at the alien, only to land headfirst in the snow. "Let me go! Let me help her!" he yelled, punching at the air where Mesmo stood. It was useless, of course. Ben gasped for air and let himself drop to the ground. He sobbed into his hands.

"We'll save her," Mesmo said sternly. "But not now. Not like this. We have to get you as far away as possible from the police, find cover, and wait out the storm."

Ben's cheeks were wet with tears. "No!" He felt like a small child who would not listen to reason.

Mesmo crouched beside him. "You must!"

Ben stared at the alien, his mind whirling. His heart couldn't bear to think of his mother spending another minute with Bordock, but his mind knew it was inevitable, for now.

He glared bitterly at Mesmo, then picked up Tike, tucked him back into his jacket, and stepped into the darkness.

CHAPTER EIGHTEEN

Acceptance

Even Mesmo's skill was not enough to keep Ben safe from the blizzard. Night had fallen, making it impossible to see far ahead. Mesmo cleared a path before Ben and kept him dry, but even so, the danger that they could be walking beside a precipice without even knowing it became too much of a risk.

Finally, Mesmo stopped before a cluster of rocks and trees. He placed his hands in the snow and swiftly melted a hole into the ground. Ben watched him disappear into the makeshift cave until he reappeared and nodded for the boy to enter. Ben bent through the doorway and found himself in a large, dry igloo below the snow.

"Take off your jacket and snow boots so I can dry them," Mesmo ordered.

Ben did so numbly. He was shivering uncontrollably, but not from the cold. He was in shock about what had happened, and he could not shake the image of his mother trudging through the blizzard at Bordock's mercy.

"Here." He heard Mesmo's voice in the dark and saw the alien's hand emit a blue light above the jacket. "You can lie down on it. You should be warm enough."

Ben sat and watched as Mesmo sealed off the doorway, leaving them in silence. He wrapped his arms around his legs and tried to calm his breathing.

"Don't worry." Mesmo's voice said through the dark. "Bordock may be evil, but he is also smart. He won't let anything happen to your mother. There is nothing more we can do but wait for the storm to blow over. He knows we will try to get off the mountain and will follow us."

"I'm not getting off the mountain," Ben interrupted. "Not without Mom."

"You're not thinking straight," Mesmo responded. "As soon as the weather clears, the police will swarm the area. And you may not have noticed yet, but you have no food."

Ben's stomach growled at the word and he squeezed his knees tighter.

"Try and get some rest," Mesmo said quietly. "I'll keep watch."

Ben lay down reluctantly, holding on to Tike's warm body as the dog snuggled up to him.

A thousand images flipped through his mind and he

clung to one of Kimi's smiling face. He pulled out the dreamcatcher she had given him and felt the soft web of strings under his fingertips. *Being born with two cultures is a gift, not a burden.* For some reason, her words echoed in his mind. She had lashed out at being half First Nation but then had come to realize her difference was her strength, not her weakness. The idea wouldn't let Ben go. He twisted uncomfortably on the snowy bed Mesmo had made him, knowing, somehow, that those words applied to him, too. Acceptance was inevitable and part of him longed to embrace it, to feel confident and steadfast in his new identity, the way he had witnessed Kimi's transformation.

But the sickness?

He pushed the thought to the back of his mind. There was no time to think about that.

"Mesmo?" Ben's voice pierced the darkness.

"Yes?"

"I want you to teach me about the skill."

There was a long pause, then Mesmo said, "Are you sure?"

Ben sighed in resignation. "Yes." He felt Mesmo approach.

"Why this change of heart?"

Ben stared at the invisible ceiling. "Because it could save Mom," he said.

✳ ✳ ✳

Laura woke to clanging sounds. She opened her eyes in a hurry and found the Shapeshifter sitting on a rock opposite her, rummaging through her backpack. He fished out a can of ravioli, a swiss knife, and a plastic spoon. With little effort, he unscrewed the top and began gobbling up the cold contents.

Laura couldn't help staring at the alien, for the bald man named Connelly who had caught her the night before, was no longer there. In his place sat Bordock: a man of muscular build, shorter than Mesmo, though with the same olive-coloured skin and white hair, which spiked out of his head like hedgehog quills.

He must have felt her gaze because he turned her way. She caught her breath and closed her eyes, but he wasn't fooled.

"Wakey, wakey," he said. "Time to get up. We have a long day ahead."

Laura gave up pretending to sleep and struggled to sit, remembering that her hands were cuffed together before her. *How convenient that he's a police officer*, she seethed silently.

She looked out of their rudimentary shelter, which Bordock had found below some jutting rocks the night before. It had been enough to prevent snow from swirling inside and he had even managed to light a small fire. Still, the night had been long and cold, and by the headache that hammered in the back of her head, Laura guessed she hadn't slept much.

"It's still snowing," she pointed out.

"Yes, but it is also daytime. Which means it's time to go."

"Go where?"

"Down the mountain, of course," Bordock said, munching. Laura tried to ignore her grumbling stomach. Bordock dug into the can of ravioli and said with a full mouth, "We have to get there before they do. We're the welcoming team, see?" He waved an empty spoon at her.

Laura glared at him. "You won't get away with this. Mesmo will crush you."

Bordock burst out laughing. Laura felt fire rise to her cheeks. "Poor little Earthling. Still thinks the friendly alien will save her." Using his tongue, he cleaned out the piece of meat stuck in his teeth, then threw the can at her. It cluttered to the ground. The spoon fell out and ravioli spilled everywhere. Laura picked it up in disgust and stared at the few remaining pasta cushions that plastered the very bottom of the can.

The alien pointed his index finger at her. "Let's get one thing straight. That Toreq scum doesn't care about you. All he cares about is the translation skill. Get this through your little brain. It's not your son he's protecting. It's the skill!"

Laura choked on the ravioli she had managed to extract from the can with her fingers.

Bordock stared at her in amazement. "Don't you realize that yet? Do you really think he's out there looking for you? He doesn't care where you are. He doesn't care whether you're alive or dead. Right now, all he's interested in is escaping these mountains with your son as fast as he can."

Laura's appetite was gone. She dropped the can to the ground. "You're lying," she said with an effort.

Bordock shrugged. He bent to gather their things and shove them into the backpack. "I know the Toreq better than you do. Trust me when I tell you, it's the skill he wants."

"...and you don't?" Laura said in a low voice, launching an accusing glare his way. To her horror, he turned slowly and smirked.

"Yes, all right," he admitted, plopping down on the rock again. "I can't deny the translation skill would be a valuable asset to my collection. But at least I'm honest about it."

Laura shuddered, thinking of Mesmo's wife. "You see, that's where you and Mesmo differ. He would never forcefully take someone's skill from them."

The corner of Bordock's mouth lifted in half a smile. "Ah, I see Mesmo has told you how I became a Shapeshifter."

Laura watched him heave the backpack onto his shoulders. Her heart sank as she realized he knew very well she couldn't survive on her own without it.

"What can I say?" he said as he fished out a tiny key from his pocket. "War comes fraught with sacrifices."

"What war?" she chided. "The War of the Kins happened millennia ago. And you lost. He told me so."

A funny smile crept into Bordock's face, one she did not like at all.

"Strange..." he said thoughtfully, releasing one of her hands, then attaching the empty cuff to his own wrist. "...strange that he should open up to you, yet tell you only half the story..." he trailed off.

"What story?"

The weird smile crept on to his face again. He shook his head. "No," he said as if speaking to himself. "No. It would be a lot more fun to watch him tell you."

He turned and pulled her away from their rocky shelter.

"Tell me what?" she insisted.

"Enough!" he snapped, making her cringe. She did not like the way his eyes had hardened. "If you want to see your son again before Mesmo takes him away, you'll want to get down this mountain as soon as possible."

Laura struggled behind him with the faintest glimmer of hope blossoming in her mind. From Bordock's last phrase, she gathered that he was not aware of Mesmo's current condition. Mesmo was reduced to a mere apparition. He could not physically force Ben to go anywhere.

Ben woke to a ray of light that shone in his left eye.

He blinked and gathered his bearings, then remembered where he was.

Faint daylight seeped through cracks in the makeshift igloo. Tike scratched at its snowy surface, making some of it crumble. The terrier trotted back to the boy to check that Ben was satisfied with him.

Ben stared at his dog as if seeing him for the first time.

Can you hear me?

The blood rushed to his ears as soon as he directed the question at Tike with his mind. The dog wagged his tail vigorously.

Of course, I can! What took you so long?

Ben shrank back into the snowy wall. He willed himself not to think anything for a moment, but the connection was crystal-clear in his mind. The part of him that was Tike, was overly thrilled and happy, while the part of his brain that was still his own was more cautious. An image of blue filaments flashed through his mind, but he pushed it away before he could panic. There was no time to think about that. He had to master the skill if he was going to help his mother—even if it meant losing himself to it.

What's wrong? Are you still angry at me?

Tike's words were unmistakable as, for the first time, Ben opened up to them entirely. It also meant feeling all of his dog's feelings, and he realized just how much he had hurt his companion in the past weeks by ignoring him.

Oh, Tike!

He picked up the terrier and hugged him.

I'm so sorry I was mean to you. I'm an idiot!

Tike licked his face.

No, you're not. I love you.

Ben was taken aback by such innocent sincerity. He hugged his dog harder.

I love you, too!

They stayed close like that for a long moment, Ben stroking Tike's back and Tike kissing him in the neck with his snout.

Light poured into the igloo as the snow melted and Mesmo appeared in the open doorway. "Benjamin?" he called. "Time to go. It's a long way down. I'm hoping to reach the road by tomorrow morning."

"After we've saved Mom."

"Right."

"Before that you have to teach me to use the skill."

Mesmo didn't answer right away. "First, let's get this day over. I need you to save your strength."

"I'm fine," Ben reassured him, before noticing the emptiness in his stomach.

Mesmo must have noticed his face change, because he said, "Time to go."

Ben stepped out of the igloo and caught his breath. Though it was still snowing, the clouds were high and grey in the sky, allowing him a glimpse of the vast landscape ahead of him. The steep Kananaskis Mountains sloped dangerously before leveling out into the plains that crossed half of Canada. Somewhere, down below, a road followed the mountain and rejoined the highway. Ben suddenly understood Mesmo's urgency. If another storm hit, he could be stuck here for days without food. Ignoring his hunger, he stepped after Mesmo as they began their descent.

CHAPTER NINETEEN

Grizzly

Ben fell headlong in the snow.

"Benjamin?" Mesmo called, hurrying to his side.

Ben turned his head but was too weak to flip onto his back.

"Get up! You have to keep going!" Mesmo urged.

"Can't," Ben muttered. He had walked for seven hours straight and he was exhausted.

Mesmo melted some snow by his mouth. "Drink!" he ordered.

Ben obeyed, feeling the fresh water flow down to his empty stomach. The descent had been brutal, especially when Mesmo had had to cut the connection with the spirit portal to return to his physical body, leaving Ben on his own for several hours. Ben's progress had been excruciatingly slow during that time because Mesmo had not been there to melt the snow in his path.

Fortunately, sometime after two o'clock, the alien had returned, allowing Ben to make good progress.

But now, Ben was done. He needed rest. And he needed food.

"You can't stay out here in the open," Mesmo said with his back to the boy. "Come on. You need to make it to the edge of the forest at least."

Ben raised his head slightly.

What forest?

He spotted it way below.

I can't.

Yes, you can. Get up!

Tike was by his side. Ben stared at his dog, whose exhaustion was more palpable even than his own. Ben felt a pang of guilt and picked himself up. Then he grabbed Tike and covered him under his jacket. His dog sent him a wave of gratitude, giving him the energy he needed to clamber down to the forest.

Ben, Mesmo and Tike made it to the border of trees by early evening. The boy collapsed in the igloo that Mesmo melted out for him and fell into a troubled sleep. His dreams bordered on hallucinations. He shivered from cold in spite of the protective snow-womb he lay in, the low temperatures having anchored themselves to his clothes. Sometimes he was talking to Tike, other times he was calling Mesmo's name, but he couldn't tell if the alien was there or not. He dug his mouth into a juicy steak, only to realize it was made of thin air, and he woke to his stomach grumbling painfully.

By morning, he couldn't shake off the fuzziness in his brain and his eyes blacked out for a second as he tried to sit up. His legs felt like numb stumps. He rubbed his face with his hands to try and get rid of his exhaustion, then broke out of his snowy shelter.

The sun shone, warming his cheeks. He lay in the snow, half-in and half-out of the igloo, unable to move. Finally, he attempted to stand shakily, his legs feeling like stubborn logs. He scanned the barren landscape with his eyes. There was no sign of Mesmo.

Having nothing better to do, Ben followed Tike as the dog wandered off into the trees. It wasn't long before they reached the edge of a lake. Ben knelt at its edge and broke a hole in the ice. Tike lapped at the water thirstily while Ben struck at the ice to make a second hole. He plunged his cracked lips into the icy liquid, ignoring its stinging cold. Somewhat satisfied at having filled his stomach with something, the boy wiped his mouth with the back of his hand.

Tike tensed beside him. The dog crouched to the ground suddenly, ears laid back, teeth barred.

Ben froze with his arm half-way up to his mouth. A low growl reached his ears, chilling his blood. Filled with a sense of foreboding, he turned to face the source of the menacing sound.

A grizzly bear towered a few feet behind him. Its mouth bristled with saliva. Its nostrils huffed. It shook its robust body, making its shaggy coat sway to-and-fro. The beast sniffed at the air, then rose on its hind legs and let out a furious roar, displaying its sharp teeth.

Ben scampered back in terror. His brain exploded with stars, the blood rushed to his ears and instantly, he was pulled into the grizzly's mind. He saw himself through the eyes of the bear with a powerful sense of irritation at the sight of this insignificant, trembling creature before him.

You trespass!

The words boomed in Ben's mind. The beast shook its mane to show off its power and might and the small creature shrank into a ball of fear before it. This only made the grizzly angrier. It wanted to swipe at the thing with one mighty paw.

A tiny part of Ben's mind was still his.

I must give in to the skill, now!

It was imperative. It was critical. His survival depended on it.

For Mom.

He let go willingly. He resigned to the translation skill and instantly slipped into the bear's thoughts, the words he needed forming in his mind's eye.

Yes! I trespass! This is your domain, mighty one. Forgive me.

The bear fell back down to its front paws in bewilderment. It sniffed at the air, trying to decide whether the insignificant creature was a menace.

Ben crouched on the ground, making himself as

small as possible. He pushed aside his feelings of fear and made the bear aware that he was completely harmless. He bent his head, avoiding eye contact, and reached out a glowing hand in submission.

The grizzly blew angrily through its nostrils, but its curiosity was piqued. It spoke with a deep, authoritative voice.

You kill my family with thunder. You steal my food. I do not like your kind.

Ben knew it was referring to hunters. He also knew it was no use lying. His mind was open to the bear, just as much as the bear's was to him.

Yes, my species can be unkind. But I am just a cub. I have no thunder. I do not like thunder.

He remained silent, allowing the beast to scan his mind, ignoring a surge of nausea.

You are strange, different. Not like the others.

Ben bit his lip.

That is because I speak your language. I can listen and obey your will.

The bear relaxed slightly and took a step back.

Ben dared lift his head to peek at the animal. It observed him curiously, deciding Ben wouldn't make a worthy meal after all. Instead, its threatening mood fell away and it was replaced by compassion.

You are hungry.

The bear could read his every feeling.

No cub in my domain goes hungry!

The grizzly lurched forward, making Ben jump. But

it headed straight for the lake. Ben watched, awestruck, as the majestic creature waded into the water, scanning the depths for fish.

Not long after, Ben plodded through the snow, away from the lake, through the forest, and out into the sun. A sleepy corner of his brain knew that he was still submerged with the bear, at the animal's complete mercy. He spotted a movement a little way off. The intrusion of another being in the bear's territory angered him and he advanced with determination.

The being had flimsy arms and legs, and fur on its small head. The being turned to face Ben the Bear and looked straight at him. "Benjamin? What's wrong?" it said, frowning.

Why do you call me Benjamin? Why do you not fear me?

Confusion entered Ben's thoughts.

Am I not a bear? What am I?

A part of his mind detached itself and became that of a boy. Ben's awareness slowly replaced the bear's thoughts as it focused on the being.

I know you.

"Ben!" Mesmo urged. "Snap out of it!"

Ben's mind uncurled entirely from that of the grizzly, which had remained by the lake, and through a hazy fog in his mind, he remembered who he was. He looked down, expecting to see huge paws, but instead found that he had hands, and that he was carrying a large trout. He let the fish slip to the ground.

I'm not a grizzly. I'm a human boy.

He stared at Mesmo in utter confusion. "Grizzly," he muttered. Then everything swam before his eyes, and he fell into darkness.

When he woke again, Ben found himself lying on his back in the snow. He turned his head, but when he did, his stomach heaved, and he retched. Nothing came out of his mouth as he had not eaten in two days. He found Mesmo staring at him intently. He remained on his side, panting, holding Mesmo's eyes as if they were anchors. His mind was free from the bear's thoughts. He was just Ben again. But fear paralyzed him. He had used the skill and it had knocked him out, making him weak and nauseous. It took a while before he found enough strength to speak. "Am I going to die?" he breathed.

Mesmo studied him with deeply knitted brows. He approached Ben and knelt beside him. "No, Benjamin Archer, you are not going to die."

Ben rolled to his side, ignoring the dizziness in his head. "Then why is the skill making me so sick?"

Mesmo's gaze bore into him. The alien's shoulders sagged as if a great burden had been placed on them, and Ben thought he saw the shadow of a deep sadness pass before his eyes. "It is not you who is sick," Mesmo said. "It is the animals."

Ben stared at the alien in stunned silence. The words repeated in his mind.

It's not me. It's the animals!

He was dumbfounded at their meaning. "But how?"

Mesmo wrung his hands together. "I have thought about it, ever since you mentioned the symptoms the first time. I thought perhaps your body was adapting to the skill, but soon it became clear that something else was going on—something that, as far as I know, has never been recorded by previous Observers of my kind. There is only one explanation: when you use the skill, you experience the animal's illness. That is my conclusion." He held Ben's gaze and asked, "Do you agree?"

Ben caught his breath. As soon as Mesmo had uttered the question, everything became evident in his head, as if a veil had lifted. And he knew, deep in his heart, that Mesmo was right. "Yes," he said in agreement. He pushed himself into a sitting position, his eyes never leaving Mesmo's gaze, and repeated, "Yes!"

His nausea was replaced by horror at the seriousness of the discovery. "But Mesmo," he gasped. "It's all of them! All the animals: the seals, the bear, the ants..." He broke off, unable to continue. The implication was staggering.

Mesmo nodded and Ben knew instinctively that the alien had reached this conclusion some time ago.

"But it doesn't make sense," Ben reflected. "They don't act sick."

"I don't think they are aware they are sick. I think it

is more like a hidden cancer that has not yet declared itself," Mesmo said. "When you connect with the creatures, you are not only communicating with them, you are also entering their whole being. You become one with them. Your body and your mind synchronize with their bodies and their minds. My daughter did that, too, when she was a small child and did not understand her skill. Where I come from, it is against the law to take over a creature's mind and body without their consent. The translation skill is used for communication only, and only if the creature is willing to communicate. The trick is to refrain from using the skill's full power unless the creature agrees to it.

"Because you are new to this skill, you have not yet learned to separate yourself from the creature. You become one with them. You forget yourself. The problem is, when your body synchronizes with theirs, it picks up any illness they may have, and its symptoms translate into your body. Hence your physical reactions.

"You are strong. You are healthy. But if you don't learn to disconnect yourself from the creatures you communicate with, your body may not recognize the difference between you and them anymore, and it will keep the symptoms. And, yes, then you truly will be sick."

Ben listened to Mesmo speak and knew that everything he said was true. It was as if some part of him had always known things were this way, but he had not known how to distinguish the animals' feelings from his own. He had connected with his whole being with many creatures already, and he shuddered when he remembered how sick he had felt after synchronizing with each of them.

He was afraid to hear the answer but needed to ask the question. "Mesmo, why are the animals sick?"

Mesmo considered him for a moment, then replied, "I think you already know."

Ben did. "Are we–humans–making them sick?"

Mesmo did not need to answer.

"But how's that possible?" Ben blurted. "We're miles away from any city. There's no pollution here. How could that bear be sick?"

Mesmo replied, "Humans are not only poisoning the cities. Pollution is seeping into the air and the water, which carries it to all corners of the globe. No mountain or ocean has been spared. I have felt it in the water, everywhere I have travelled. This poison has been absorbed by all the living creatures on this planet. It is lying in wait in their bones, in their blood. If nothing is done soon, this terminal illness will declare itself and a massive extinction will be unchained among the animal kingdom. I fear none will be spared, perhaps not even humans."

Ben gaped. The enormity of this revelation was almost too much to bare. He thought of the gentle giant, the humpback whale, who had taken him into the deep ocean for a brief instant. And the seals, who had wanted to play with him under the surface of the water. Poisoned by his own species.

I can't let that happen!

In that instant, something was born inside of Ben, like a calling or a lifelong purpose, and he knew things would never be the same again. A sudden realization came to him. "Is that why you came to Earth? To save the animals from dying out?"

A strange look crossed Mesmo's face—one that he could not read. The alien stood and said, "You need to eat." He placed his hands in the snow and melted it, so it covered the trout that the grizzly had offered Ben.

Ben stood as well, joining Mesmo hastily. "I want to help! I understand everything now. I want to master the skill and help you save the animals."

Mesmo did not seem to share his enthusiasm. He smiled, but his eyes remained sad. "You can't do that on an empty stomach," he said. "I know you said you want to become a vegetarian, but right now I think you need to break your vow."

Ben watched as bubbles and steam appeared on the surface of the water, rising from under the trout. A delicious smell seeped from the fumes. "You're boiling the fish?" he asked in wonder.

Mesmo smiled. "I can't light a fire, so this will have to do."

Ben's mouth watered and he forgot about his questions.

CHAPTER TWENTY

Convergence

Laura stumbled after Bordock in a daze. She wanted to lie down and drift into a deep sleep, but the idea that Ben might be alone on the mountain kept her going. She prayed that Mesmo had not abandoned him, though she knew that, considering his condition, it would be impossible for him to remain at Ben's side at all times. He would have to return to his physical body at some point.

Her mouth dried at the thought that Mesmo could betray them somehow; that he was in fact the enemy. She could not, would not, believe it. Bordock was the one who had killed Mesmo's wife and daughter, shot down Mesmo's spacecraft and threatened Ben. She hated his ability to plant doubt in her mind and she pictured him as a deceitful chameleon that changed colours according to what suited him best.

Bordock pulled at her numb arm to keep going. She faintly registered that they were marching along a dense forest of fir trees.

Then a sound reached her ears. She forced herself to pay attention, as her fuzzy mind could not determine what it was.

Bordock stopped and they both listened as the rumbling drew nearer at incredible speed.

Suddenly, Laura identified the source of the noise. "Helicopter!" she shouted.

Bordock pulled her away from the clearing and into the forest. He pushed her between some thick roots and held her down until the helicopter had zoomed over their heads.

Laura regained complete consciousness in an instant. Her heart drummed in her chest. She risked a peek into the clearing and spotted a couple of helicopters the size of flies high up on the mountain. The sky had turned blue, with scattered white clouds. Before long the area would be crawling with search teams.

Bordock grabbed her wrist and dragged her deeper into the forest until they reached the edge of a small lake, hidden under the branches of the trees. They stopped again, breathing hard, listening to the muffled silence.

This time it was not a sound that caught their attention. It was a smell. The smell of cooking fish: unexpected and penetrating.

"Smells like breakfast," Bordock smirked.

Laura's eyes widened. They were both thinking the same thing.

"Ben!" she gasped in horror.

Instantly, Bordock had a key in his hand. He unlocked the cuff on his arm and dragged her to a young birch tree.

"No, wait!" she yelled, fighting him. He was too strong and in no time had passed her arms around the tree trunk and closed the handcuff around her other wrist. Then he was off, following the direction of the smell.

"No!" she shouted, struggling to free herself. "Ben! Ben!"

✳ ✳ ✳

Ben had gobbled up half the trout when the helicopter came. He plunged into the igloo with Mesmo just before it roared over their heads. He listened to the main-rotor blade cutting through the air until long after it was gone.

Carefully, he and Mesmo extracted themselves from the snowy shelter and checked their surroundings.

"Up there," Mesmo said, pointing to the Kananaskis peaks. Helicopters were circling an area high up the mountain which Ben judged was where they had left the pick-up truck. "Time to go," Mesmo urged.

"What about Mom?" Ben asked in alarm. Now that

his hunger was stilled, his brain was sharp as a tack.

"Don't worry, we'll find her," Mesmo answered.

Really?

Ben put on his snow jacket slowly, struggling with doubt.

A crow hopped over and stole a bit of fish, which did not please Tike. The dog made as if to attack it, and it flew back a few feet, cawing indignantly. Tike went back to gnawing at the fish bones, eyeing the bird suspiciously.

"Hey, I know you!" Ben said, startled.

You're the crow with a broken wing.

Inevitably, Ben's blood swirled in his ears and already he felt himself drawn to the bird.

"Not now, Ben," Mesmo warned.

"Yes, now!" Ben spoke sharply. "This might be the only chance I get to find my mom." He glared at the alien, challenging him to object.

Mesmo scanned the sky rigidly. "All right," he said. "But be quick. And ask for permission first, and don't lose yourself in the creature. Remember who you are."

Ben nodded. "Move away, Tike," he said. "Let our friend have some."

In his mind, he heard the dog growl as he moved away with the fish's tail in his jaw. The crow approached them again, then helped itself to another small piece of trout skin.

Ben hunched down next to it.

Hello, I am Benjamin Archer. Do you remember me?

The crow eyed him with beady eyes.

Greetings, Benjamin Archer. I am Corbilyn. Yes, I remember you.

Ben breathed in sharply. He had just approached the skill in a new way. He checked Corbalyn's wing, reminding himself that the crow was a she.

How is your wing?

It has healed well. You saved me. You may ask any favour of me.

I'm glad you are better. And I do have a favour to ask. I seek my mother. She is in danger.

I know where she is. I will take you. You may come.

Immediately, Ben felt drawn into the crow, and for a second he forgot who he was. But then he remembered Mesmo's words and gently rested his mind's eye on the crow's back.

I am still Ben.

He managed to keep control of his thoughts, instead of being swallowed up body and mind into the bird.

Corbalyn took off and soared above the trees, leaving a tiny Mesmo, Ben and Tike behind. The Ben whose spirit was flying with the crow watched as the physical Ben crumbled to the ground below him. He was not worried. A sense of exhilaration made his mind soar with the bird. The earth fell away beneath him revealing an immense landscape covered in a blanket of pristine snow. The mountains towered to his left; to his right, plains stretched as far as his mind's eyes could see. The air was gentle and fresh on the bird's wings. Ben's soul experienced a moment of utter happiness, and for the first time, he understood that the skill was indeed a gift. He told the crow, *Thank you!*

The bird swooped to the right, passing a large patch of snow that rolled down to a shimmering river at the bottom of the mountain. Several dots moved on it, and with a start, Ben realized that it was not a river, but a road.

We're almost there!

He smiled inwardly at the thought that escape was near.

Now to find my mother.

She is here.

Corbalyn glided down to a forest not far from Ben's shelter. The small lake where the grizzly had caught the trout came into view, and Ben's adrenaline increased when he caught a movement in the trees. He spotted his mother and panic careened through his mind. Corbalyn landed on a branch in alarm.

Below them, Laura fought to free herself from a tree trunk, shouting in panic, "Ben! Ben!"

"Are you sure this is a good idea?" Hao asked.

He struggled to place one foot in front of the other as, each time, he sank knee deep in the snow. Below him, the lights of half a dozen police cars whirled, stationed at the edge of the road, at the bottom of the Kananaskis. Hao believed they were miles away from where they should be.

"We've got the mountaintop covered," the Sheriff said as if reading his thoughts. "If they survived the storm, they will be heading this way. We'll comb the area from the road upwards, and the helicopters will do the same from the top down."

A dozen officers followed Hao and the Sheriff as they headed through the forest.

This is going to be a long day, Hao thought. He clenched his teeth as he trudged on. He still couldn't believe that Connelly had been foolish anough to follow the fugitives into a raging snowstorm. High Inspector Tremblay had been furious—as if Connelly's stupidity had been Hao's fault.

Hao mulled over the unfair situation—focusing on his anger rather than on the rugged terrain—when an officer yelled a warning. He tensed, eyes alert, scanning the trees for signs of danger. Then he saw it, a movement in the trees, a giant shadow lumbering at an uncomfortably close distance.

"Grizzly!" the Sheriff cautioned.

With a swift motion, Hao pulled the gun from his side and aimed.

"Whoa!" the Sheriff yelled. "What do you think you're doing?" He yanked Hao's arm down so the gun was pointing at the ground.

"For goodness sake!" Hao snapped. "You just said: that's a grizzly!"

The Sheriff shook his head as if Hao was a small child. "You aren't from around here. The dangers aren't where you think they are. First, if you shoot, there is a high chance you will injure the bear. Trust me, you do not want to irritate a grizzly. Second, we just had a snowstorm in early spring, which is melting as we speak. A shot like that could trigger an avalanche and that would be ten times worse than a charging bear." He let go of Hao's arm. "Believe me, it's best to leave it alone."

Hao watched as the brown animal disappeared into the forest. "So, how, exactly, are we supposed to defend ourselves? Do you really think those fugitives are going to run into our arms willingly?"

The Sheriff sighed and shrugged. "Guns are for last resort only." He signalled to his men to move forward.

Hao put away his side arm but kept his hand close to it. The memory of an attack by another massive animal—the humpback whale—was still fresh in his mind. The Sheriff had no idea what they were up against, and Hao wasn't going to let himself be fooled twice.

CHAPTER TWENTY-ONE

Confrontation

Ben's mind did a double flip at his mother's cries, his thoughts getting entwined with that of the crow.

Stop it!

Corbalyn struggled.

Ben couldn't make sense of who he was anymore. He wanted to speak. He tried to use his voice to reassure Laura, but all that came out were exasperated caws.

Corbalyn took off.

No, wait!

Ben was powerless under the crow's will as it flew back to the snowy shelter. As it prepared to dive, Ben's inner eye caught Bordock hiding behind a tall fir tree, his hands glowing with intense power, ready to strike.

Dread shot through Ben's mind like lightning,

making Corbalyn lurch. Unable to control her movements, the crow fell in a messy heap to the ground. With superhuman effort, Ben tore himself from the bird's mind. Full consciousness returned to his body at once. He swallowed cold air through his mouth with a loud gasp as his eyes shot open.

"B-o-r-d-o-c-k!" he shouted.

Too late.

Bordock thrust the mysterious power from his hands and it swept at them like a whip, hitting Mesmo first but avoiding Ben whose body still sprawled on the ground.

Mesmo vanished.

The trunk from the fully mature fir tree next to Bordock detached itself from its base with a loud crunch. It teetered, then plummeted towards Ben who watched in dismay.

A deep thud resonated on the mountain as it hit the ground. The branches plastered the snow, releasing a sprinkle of pine needles in the air as they swayed. Static dissipated slowly, a remnant from the alien impact. Then everything went silent.

Ben's breath came out in rapid gasps. He peeked carefully from behind his arms and found thick branches a foot from his face. Twigs had scraped his cheeks and a strong smell of earth filled his nostrils. But he was unharmed.

He daren't move, his heart fluttered, while he took in the protective cocoon of branches that could have killed him had he been lying a little to the right. A light sense of claustrophobia enveloped him under the stuffy branches.

I need to get out.

The regular, crunching sound of footsteps in the snow froze him to the spot.

Bordock!

He peeked through the branches and saw the shapeshifter moving slowly along the tree. Ben scrambled backwards, using his elbows and feet to push himself further away, but Bordock must have heard him, because he stopped and straightened.

"Well, well," the alien said. "A spirit portal. How convenient. As soon as our Toreq friend senses danger, he zaps away to safety."

Ben watched Bordock bend and search under the branches. The boy remained still as stone, hardly daring to breathe.

"I find that very disappointing," Bordock continued, lifting another branch. "Don't you?" He let go of the branch and stepped slowly along the fringe of the tree, causing Ben to scamper under its trunk for refuge. He shut his eyes tight and prayed that the shapeshifter would walk by him.

"You and I are more alike than you know," Bordock said, his voice too close for comfort. "Think about it. Both of us were born without a Toreq skill." His footsteps paused. "And someone had to die for us to inherit one."

Ben placed his hands firmly on his mouth. Images of a fading Kaia flashed before his eyes and he wanted to scream. Yes, she had died after she had given her skill to him, but he had not taken it from her forcefully.

We are not alike!

"Huh," Bordock said with interest, his voice moving away. "There's your dog. I hope it's not hurt." His footsteps receded.

Ben's eyes shot open.

Tike!

His hands began to glow and blood rushed to his ears. He listened, but there was only silence.

Tike?

He called his dog with his mind, anxiously trying to make contact. There was no answer.

Ben's heart leapt. He turned to lie on his stomach and pulled himself frantically through the snow with his arms.

I'm right here. I'm stuck.

Branches rustled not far from Ben and he found the terrier trapped in a natural cage made of twigs laden with pine needles.

"Hold on..." Ben whispered, reaching out to release his dog. "Aargh!"

A firm hand grabbed the boy forcefully by the collar. He yelled, struggling as Bordock dragged him on his back into the open. Ben's arms flailed, searching for something to grab on to but his hands only found snow. Frantic, he raised his arms and let himself slide out of his jacket.

Bordock whirled.

Ben sprang to his feet, but the alien was too close for

him to be able to make a run for it. He staggered backwards, Bordock shadowing his every step.

"We are *not* alike!" Ben burst out with a mixture of anger and fear.

A sliver of a smile appeared on Bordock's face. "Ah, but we are. If only you would stop running and let me explain. We could get your mother. We could sit down, the three of us, and talk. She is not far. I took good care of her. You can trust me." He reached out his hand.

Ben's heart leapt in disgust. "You're lying! I saw her—in there." He pointed to the forest behind them, vaguely surprised that his hands were still blue from connecting with Tike. "I'll never trust you!" he said, taking another step back. His foot caught in something. He tripped and fell heavily on his backside.

In a flash, Bordock was on top of him, choking him with his hands. "Clever boy," he said with a growl.

Ben squirmed. The more he struggled, the more Bordock pressed on his neck, until he saw stars. He grabbed Bordock's arms weakly, his hands gleaming from the skill.

Bordock nodded satisfyingly. "Good. The skill is strong. It has lost nothing of its essence." His face was strangely calm and his eyes were emotionless black pearls. "No need to resist," he said quietly. "It won't hurt."

He waved a hand over Ben's face and Ben felt his eyes roll back in his head. In his mind's eye, he watched the blue fillaments begin to seep away from every blood cell. And it hurt. It hurt as if a million healthy teeth were being extracted at the same time. Whales, ants, crows, bears–Tike–all flashed before his eyes. It was as if his closest friends were being torn away from him.

Not the skill!

For the first and briefest moment, Ben knew he never wanted to part with the skill. It was his, and his alone, and Kaia had seen it in him that he was worthy to wield it.

Determination broke through the pain and Ben focused the strength he had left towards the skill. He sensed his hands glowing ever stronger and the blood in his ears rushed like waterfalls. Yet that action only made it easier for Bordock to absorb the skill like a magnet.

There was a scuffle, and Ben heard a short yelp. The connection broke for a fraction of a second. It was all Ben needed. The skill exploded outwards. His mind's eye caught Tike biting Bordock's arm and Bordock casting the dog away. He sent one thought whizzing on through the forest until it collided with the mind of the grizzly.

H-E-L-P!

No sooner had he uttered the silent cry than Ben's world turned dark again. Bordock reaped the blue fillaments from the boy's blood cells, destroying them in the process. Ben knew he was done for.

He felt himself fall into a tunnel of darkness .He floated in a murky world for an obscure amount of time, watching helplessly as the skill floated away from him.

From somewhere beyond his closed eyelids, he watched with numb interest as a gigantic shadow swooped over him.

There was a deafening roar and a shriek.

And just like that, Bordock was gone.

Ben gasped, the air leaving his throat in rasps. He blinked his eyes open, forced himself painfully on his stomach and watched, dumbfounded, as the grizzly bear held Bordock in its paws.

A mighty bang escaped from the alien's hands, thrusting the two away from each other. The grizzly collapsed on its side. Bordock crouched not far from it like a wounded animal.

Abruptly, Mesmo appeared out of nowhere. He placed his hands in the snow and a wall of ice surged before them, separating them from the shapeshifter.

Ben staggered to the grizzly's side. He searched the bear's mind frantically, his throat on fire.

Are you hurt?

He scanned the bear as it huffed heavily through its nostrils.

I am fine. Run, little cub. The men with thunder are here.

An image of whirling police car lights flashed through Ben's mind. He caught his breath, consumed by an immediate sense of urgency.

He turned to Mesmo, who was staring at the icy wall he had created. The alien's face was pale and grey. Whatever Bordock's attack had done to him, it had left a mark.

The shapeshifter stalked them from behind the ice,

surrounded by a halo of blue light. Something abnormal was happening to the outline of his body. It twisted and deformed, inflating like a balloon.

Ben's mouth dropped as he realized the alien's intentions.

He's turning into a grizzly!

Ben and Mesmo watched, stunned, as the shape of a grizzly bear, identical to Ben's friend, took form behind the ice. The dark creature contemplated them with a low, menacing growl. Then it moved away swiftly, taking them off guard.

Ben's pulse raced as he realized Bordock's intentions. "My mom! He's going after my mom!"

They sprang into action.

"Tike, hurry!" Ben called his dog as they sprinted into the trees after the shapeshifter.

By the time they reached the edge of the lake, the fake grizzly had already gained the other side. Mesmo plunged his hands in the half-frozen water and sharp, crystalline stalagmites shot up from its surface, forming a wall that crackled with immense, sharp edges, cutting off the grizzly's path to Laura.

Ben didn't wait to see what Bordock would do next. He raced along the far edge of the lake, taking the long way around the sharp-toothed wall. He reached his mother as she crouched by the tree, trying to protect herself from flying ice-debris from the waves of power that emanated from either alien as they battled.

"Ben!" she gasped as he threw his arms around her.

He saw the handcuffs and understood why she couldn't get away. He pulled at them, knowing it was useless. He glanced around for Mesmo and spotted the alien on the other side of the lake, catching his eye. Again, the alien hovered his hand above the surface of the lake.

"Watch out!" Ben yelled, covering his mother's head with his arms.

A silent explosion hurtled him backwards. He hit his head on a tree trunk and saw stars. Blinking several times, he saw that the lake no longer existed. It had transformed into a thick fog filled with glittering droplets of water suspended in mid-air.

Already Mesmo was at Laura's side. He surrounded the handcuffs with snow and froze it to such a degree that the metal cracked.

"Ouch!" Laura yelled when the sub-zero metal scraped her arm.

"Sorry," Mesmo apologized, but Laura was already up, kneading her wrist.

She rushed over to Ben. "Are you ok?"

Ben nodded, rubbing the back of his head.

They helped each other up and followed Mesmo hastily as he parted a way for them through the thick mist.

The officers heard the strange sounds coming from

the forest: low but powerful rumblings. Pine needless shook off the trees. Waves of cold air, not like natural gusts of wind, slapped their faces. They crouched down, glancing at each other with wide eyes.

"What's going on?" one of them asked.

Hao saw tiny, blue sparkles of ice floating by. "It's them!" He straightened and spotted a clearing some way ahead. "Let's go!" he urged.

The Sheriff spoke into his walkie-talkie, directing the helicopters towards the source of the noise.

CHAPTER TWENTY-TWO

The Wrath of the Kananaskis

Suddenly, they were out in the open.

Laura and Ben stopped at the edge of the forest, hesitating to step onto the fold of the mountain.

Ben gasped. He recognized the clearing; he had flown over it with the crow's help. "The road's over there!" He pointed to the other side of the snow-packed area. Spotting a corner of the road from where they stood, he took Laura's hand and urged her on.

She didn't budge as she scanned the area, her face tightening. "Maybe we should follow the trees..." she began, staring down the slope.

At the bottom of the mountain, Ben saw a lone man venture onto the open. Even from so far away, Ben recognized Inspector Hao. Along the side of the forest, other men slowly made their way up towards them.

A sound like firecrackers sent them flying for cover. Ben whirled to find Bordock the Grizzly emerging from the shadows of the forest. The animal's body fluctuated from an intense heat that surrounded it, its eyes gleaming a cold blue. The trees scorched black at its passage. Large branches snapped like twigs in a hurricane and fell to the ground around it. Ben felt goosebumps rise at the tension emanating from the shapeshifter. Bordock was livid.

"Go!" Mesmo yelled.

Ben and Laura sprang in the opposite direction, glancing over their shoulders.

Bordock the Grizzly glowed steadily from a blue halo of power, which he concentrated before him and thrust at them with a sway of its large head.

It was all Mesmo could do to stop the formidable attack. He erected a vast wall of ice, just in time. It curved under the force of the static blow and bent towards Ben and Laura like a massive, frozen hand rushing to engulf them.

But it was enough to sway the onslaught from Bordock's transparent wave of energy, which slipped off the arched crest like lightning and was projected skyward. The crackling static caught a passing helicopter, which was hurled aside as if a giant finger had flicked it away.

Mesmo lifted his fist from the ground at the base of the gigantic hand made of ice. Behind it, Bordock the Grizzly moved up and down like a trapped beast searching for an exit, its form visible as if through cracked glass.

Mesmo urged Ben and Laura away. They had been rooted to the spot, mesmerized by the alien confrontation. Needing no further encouragements, Ben struggled forward after his mother, their progress hampered by the deep snow.

He was almost halfway across the mountain artery when something pulled at his mind and blood rushed to his ears. A name left his lips, making him cringe with terror.

"Tike!"

Ben merged with his dog in an instant. He watched through Tike's eyes as the terrier sniffed at the icy wave Mesmo had created, searching for a way out. Finding none, the dog turned to face Bordock the Grizzly.

The shapeshifter spotted him and roared with mad fury. The electrifying fear that grasped Tike was so strong it ejected Ben from his dog's mind. The boy tumbled to the ground and watched helplessly as the beast lurched after his dog. The two animals scrambled down the mountain in a frenzy.

"Tike! No! Come back!" Ben cried.

He dove down the mountain after his dog, who scurried straight towards Hao.

Hao's blood went cold when the furious grizzly

emerged from the trees. It headed into the clearing and bolted headlong in his direction. He briefly registered the boy and his mother, then a man unexpectedly rushing after it.

What's wrong with them?

"Grizzly!" he yelled in warning to the Sheriff. He expertly seized his gun, aimed at the charging beast, and pulled the trigger. There was a deafening bang, followed by a whimper.

The boy's cry was heartwrenching.

"N-o-o-o-o-o!"

The grizzly scampered back at the deafening sound. It rushed for cover in close proximity of the trees, unharmed.

Hao watched, confused, as the boy continued to run towards him. *I thought I missed?* He saw Ben throw himself behind a mound of snow.

The grizzly shook its mane, then slowly approached again.

Hao raised his gun once more, but just then the ground heaved beneath him. His mouth fell open. A portion of the mountain detached itself, releasing an outbreak of snow, which came toppling down the slope with an unmistakable, heartstopping rumble.

"Avalanche!" The Sheriff's shout barely reached his ears above the noise. "Fall back!"

The raging snow plunged towards them, unforgiving, swallowing the grizzly, then the three fugitives.

Hao had a brief moment to think. *This was not how I expected to die*, before the avalanche caught up with him and thrust him into darkness.

Ben longed for silence. He didn't care about the overpowering noise that surrounded him, the threatening roar that resembled a furious gust of wind, the trembling ground beneath him, or the strange blue light that covered him. He didn't care about the alien who yelled under the effort to keep them safe from the raging avalanche, his hands spread out before him in an attempt to shove the descending snow above and around them. He didn't care that, when a muffled silence finally settled, the alien had almost become transparent as he staggered to the ground. Somewhere far away, his mother was calling his name. He didn't care about that either.

All Ben cared about was the heartbeat. Tike's heartbeat: very slow, very weak. Just like his. The excruciating pain that had blasted through his chest was almost too much too bear. It throbbed with each pulse, sending a flood of agony through his body. Or was it Tike's? He couldn't tell. They were one and the same. But as long as they held each other's gaze, maybe there was a chance, a glimmer of hope.

Tike blinked. A tiny light gleamed in his eyes and

Ben held on to it with all his might.

"Ben!" Mesmo's voice barely reached him. "Break the connection!" The alien's shouts were a mere irritating buzz in Ben's ear.

Don't listen to him. I'm staying with you.

It hurts!

It's ok. Give me your pain. I'll help you carry it.

Searing pain gushed through Ben's body and he groaned.

"Ben! Break the connection or you'll die!" The words were vital, pressing, yet unimportant.

"Ben! Wake up! Ben!" His mother called frantically.

Why don't they leave us alone?

Ben held his dog's gaze. It was the only thing that mattered in the world.

Laura's voice called from far away. "Tike!" Tike's eyes moved away from Ben's and the boy struggled inwardly, not wanting to break the only bridge remaining between them.

"Tike," Laura sobbed. "You beautiful, beautiful dog. Please don't take Ben away from me! You have to let him go."

Ben didn't catch the meaning of the words, but he did not like the sound of them. Tike licked Laura's hand once, then his eyes fell on Ben again.

It's ok. I feel better already. I'm going to sleep a bit now. I love you.

I love you, too.

Ben felt reassured. His dog was going to sleep for a

while. Maybe he would, too. Ben sent him a blanket of comforting thoughts, wishing his dog a good rest. They did not get through. The bridge between them faded. The light in Tike's eyes faded. Something was wrong.

No, wait!

The dog's body sagged and Ben felt a rush of consciousness return to his mind. Cold under his body, a hard roof of ice above his head, the touch of his mother's hand on his shoulder.

He swallowed a tremendous volume of air, which triggered his body functions. He heaved and wailed, "No! Tike!"

CHAPTER TWENTY-THREE

Doubt

Hao blinked his eyes open. His brain was scattered and he felt completely disoriented. He tried to move, but for some reason his body would not respond. His eyes focused and he saw white. Everything was white. He wiggled his gloves; the stuff that surrounded his fingers seeped cold through the material.

And suddenly he remembered. His body jolted at the realization. He had been caught in an avalanche. And he was trapped in it, alive.

He gasped in panic as his mind scrambled to grasp reality. Never in his life had he been more afraid.

He almost lost consciousness again, but then his years of harsh training in the police kicked in. He shut his eyes, willed his breathing to slow, and focused on forming coherent thoughts. It took him a while to quiet the horrendous thoughts of being buried under miles of snow, alone. He blocked the image out of his mind and concentrated on facts.

For one, he wasn't alone. He was confident that the Sheriff and his men had survived the avalanche, for they had been near the trees and would have had time to run for cover. One of them, at least, would rush for help.

Then, there were the helicopters. They would have seen the event from up high. Hao reassured himself with as much confidence as he could muster that help was on the way. A couple of hours at the most—that was the amount of time he would need to wait before rescue teams were set into action. He could handle a couple of hours.

Now to figure out how to catch their attention. Hao's heart skipped a beat as he realized the extent of the area they would have to search. He struggled for several minutes to restrain his reoccurring panic.

He licked his dry lips, still breathing hard, but in a more controlled way. He checked his body, moving one muscle at a time, testing for injuries. Everything seemed in one piece until he reached his left leg. A searing pain sent him yelling in shock. Black spots floated before his eyes and he puffed air like a locomotive.

"Broken leg, check."

He tried to move his hands and arms. The right one was trapped, but the left one had a bit more space. He loosened some snow with his fingers, feeling which way it fell.

At least I'm not upside down, he thought scornfully.

He moved his head to his left and caught his breath. He could see the blue sky through a small crack in the snow just above him.

"Help! Help!" he shouted before realizing it was useless. He wasn't too far from the surface. If only he could free his arm.

Painstakingly, Hao began to scratch away at the snow.

* * *

Laura cradled Ben in her arms. She had covered Tike's ruined body under her sweater. Mesmo sat with his legs bent upright, his arms resting on his knees, his head hanging in total exhaustion. Laura noticed his grey skin anxiously. Eventually, he lifted his head and said determinedly, "You can't stay here. You need to get away and find a safe place to hide. I won't be able to follow. You'll be on your own."

Laura held his gaze and fished a notebook page out of her back pocket. She scanned the five names on the small document that her father had left her.

"Bob M.?" Mesmo asked, pointing at the last name on the list.

Laura sighed, then folded the notebook page again. "Yes: Bob M.," she confirmed with a final tone in her voice, indicating she wasn't inviting any more questions. She stuffed the paper in her back pocket. "Ben needs a place to heal. We'll be heading to Toronto. Bob will help us." She lowered her gaze, burning to ask how bad his wounds were. But Bordock had shaken her faith in him.

"What is it?" Mesmo asked.

She bit her lip.

"It's Bordock, isn't it?" Mesmo pressed. "What did he tell you?"

She shot him an accusing glance. "Not enough." She could tell he was struggling to remain present and her heart ached to reassure him.

Mesmo considered her, then said quietly, "I never asked anything of you, Laura Archer. You were the one who offered to help me."

When she didn't answer, he said, "Look at me."

She did.

His honey-brown eyes did not reflect any resentment or accusation. He held her gaze and said, "I know you don't trust me. And you probably shouldn't. But there is one thing you can be certain of. I would never harm Ben." He paused to make sure she was listening. "You need to realize, I could have taken Ben's skill away from him any time. But I didn't. And I won't."

Laura swallowed and lowered her eyes in shame.

"Laura," he said, forcing her to look at him again. "You don't owe me anything. You are free to go."

She opened her mouth, but couldn't find anything to say. He stood and backed away into the wall of their icy cocoon. He placed his hands on its surface and began melting away the snow, thus creating a tunnel coated in bluish light.

If her heart had been heavy before, now it weighed like a brick. "Ben?" she said, shaking his elbow.

Ben winced and placed a hand to his chest.

Laura's face tightened with worry. She lay him down and lifted his sweater and shirt. On Ben's chest, near his heart, was a large, black-and-blue smudge that corresponded with the area where Tike had been hit. A sob escaped as she realized how close she had been to losing him.

Mesmo came back, hunched over and pale. His image faded, she could see the tunnel right through him.

"Ben, we have to go." She nudged him gently, but he remained limp in her arms. He opened his eyes and saw Tike. His face crumpled.

Laura and Mesmo exchanged a glance.

She didn't think he still had it in him, but the alien placed his hands around Tike's body. Water flowed around the terrier until it formed a block. Mesmo froze the water in such a way that it became smooth and transparent, like resistant glass.

The three of them remained there for a silent moment, watching Tike who seemed to be sleeping peacefully in his icy coffin.

✳ ✳ ✳

Hao squeezed his hand open and closed to restore some circulation to it. His gloved fingers cramped, but he was making headway. This was no time to give up. He sweated profusely and panted under the effort until he was finally able to bend his arm up to his shoulder. Next feat would be to reach his arm through the hole above his head. He decided to take a short break to calm his thoughts and rest his arm. He just wanted to close his eyes for a minute...

Cold drops splattered on his cheek. Hao woke with a start, panic surging through his body. Had he really fallen asleep? He swore angrily. His body ached from being forced into the same position for...how many hours?

How long was I asleep for? Dread overwhelmed him.

A shadow passed overhead. He twisted his head to peek through the hole, fully expecting to see a cloud or, worse, setting dusk.

Instead, he saw a man standing right above him. Hao could see the underside of his chin and his nose. The man glanced in the distance.

"Hey!" Hao shouted. "H-e-e-e-y!"

He yelled and yelled for help, but the man just stood there, impassive.

He can't hear me! Hao realized in horror. Despair gripped him.

"Help!" he said weakly, his eyes filling with tears.

The man glanced down, his bald head reflecting the late sun.

Hao blinked in a hurry. "Connelly!" he shouted frantically. "I'm down here! Help!"

Connelly seemed to be looking straight down at him, yet his face was expressionless.

Why can't he see me? Hao thought in alarm.

Something was wrong with the bald man's eyes, but he couldn't put his finger on it.

I'm delirious, Hao thought.

Connelly straightened and moved away, disappearing from his view in a second.

"No! Connelly! Come back!" Hao shouted in a strangled voice. He sobbed, unabashed, giving in to exhaustion and fear. When he finally calmed down, snippets of thoughts and images haunted his mind. Grizzlies that charged him, innocent-looking boys that transformed into alien monsters, dark spaceships hiding imminent threats...

He had not been ready for this assignment. It was beyond his human comprehension. "I just want to make sure you stop in time." His sister Lizzie's words scolded him from the border of his sanity. If only he had listened to her!

Connelly's face floated on his eyelids, strangely twisted as he stared at Hao without seeing him.

But he DID see me.

The thought jolted him awake. Hao's body shook with cold and shock, but a spark lit deep within him.

"He D-DID see m-me!" he stuttered, his eyes widening in disbelief, consciousness returning with force.

That one thought, whether originating from a hallucination or reality, sent a rush of power through his body, willing him to live. His ears caught the sound of a passing helicopter.

Using this new source of energy, Hao began to scratch frantically at the snow again. He could not feel his fingers but went on anyway, and before long, he shoved his arm through the opening above his head, sticking his hand out to the surface, like a signalling flag.

✳ ✳ ✳

On the verge of being overcome with emotion, Laura heaved Ben to his feet, placed his arm around her neck and encouraged him to walk away. He was too numb to resist and let himself be guided through the tunnel.

Mesmo closed up the tomb and, once they were out, made the snow collapse into the tunnel behind them.

The sun shone warmly on their skin from a beautiful, crisp sky. The significant flow of the avalanche was visible, and there wasn't a soul in sight, though a helicopter hovered some way up the mountain.

Laura spotted the road they had been trying to reach for two days.

Has it only been two days? she thought in wonder.

Before long, she and Ben took a place in the back of a camper of a friendly couple of skiers who were headed to the city of Calgary. Ambulances and police cars sped by them in the opposite direction, rushing to the scene of the avalanche.

As they drove off, Laura stared out the back window and saw Mesmo standing on a ledge, his form barely visible. She knew instinctively that he had gone too far. A lump formed in her throat and she realized that, friend or foe, she would end up helping him.

Victor Hayward leaned back in his chair and peeked under the business table. He didn't care whether the investors who surrounded him thought he had fallen asleep. He had stopped counting the hours since he had begun negotiating with the twenty-or-so businessmen, split evenly to his left and to his right. One of them spoke angrily, jabbing a finger at the perfectly polished oak table.

Hayward had long given up listening to the man's accusations, especially when his emergency phone buzzed, indicating something was up with the alien.

He held the phone under the table and watched the video clip his contact had sent him. The grainy black and white image that filmed the alien non-stop had captured an unmistakable scene: the alien was having seizures. The video stopped when men clad in doctor's coats and masks rushed to the alien's side.

Hayward typed hastily: WHEN?

His contact replied: 15 MIN AGO.

Hayward waited impatiently for more. When nothing came, he texted: REPORT!

His contact wrote: ALIVE. BUT BAD SHAPE.

Hayward sighed in frustration, then texted: ON MY WAY.

He put away the phone and realized that the bothersome investor was staring at him condescendingly while he continued to enumerate his grievances.

Hayward placed both his hands flat on the table, feeling the cool, soft surface on his skin. He let the investor blab away for some time, then said sharply, "Enough."

The investor barely paused in his lecture, addressing the other men at the table who were all ears.

Hayward smacked both hands loudly on the table. "Enough!" he shouted.

The investor plopped on the chair, his face turning pale as white bedsheets.

Hayward stood slowly, his imposing presence making up for his short stature.

"Enough of your whining," he seethed. "Whining never made anyone rich. Whining isn't what's going to put money back in your bank accounts." He displayed the back of his stubby hands, fingers spread out before his face. "These two hands built an empire through hard work and sweat. You wouldn't know what that means because you're just a bunch of scavengers, scrambling over each other to catch the falling crumbs. But I say, enough! I have an empire to rebuild, and I have two hands to do it with. You have delayed me far too long. I am needed at headquarters. This meeting is over."

"But the oil..." someone ventured meekly.

"Forget the oil." Hayward cut in. "Oil is a thing of the past. It is time to introduce new, boundless energy to the aviation business. Heed my words. Victory Air will be the first company in the world to introduce cutting-edge technology never heard of before."

He glared at them, all twenty investors in turn, then straightened the jacket of his business suit and headed out with a confident stride.

He paused by the door and said, "Don't forget who you're dealing with. I am Victor Hayward. Remain loyal to me and gold will roll off the table into your laps. Or else, scatter back to the filthy gutter from whence you came."

He waited until an assistant hurriedly opened the meeting room doors for him, then headed down the hall with a determined stride.

He had delayed too long. He needed answers, and he needed them now!

EPILOGUE

The crow rested on a rooftop, watching as a grey bus pulled out of a large station topped with the letters GREYHOUND STATION CALGARY. It kept its beady eyes on the boy seated with his forehead pressed against the windowpane. Their eyes met briefly before the bus turned into a bustling street.

The crow took flight, escaping the fumes coming from noisy cars and the shiny skyscrapers. It followed the sun as it descended in the sky, caressing the tips of the Canadian Rockies. Their snowy caps put on gowns of orange and red while stars began to appear in the dusk.

The crow beat its wings rhythmically, purposefully, until she found the Kananaskis Mountain Range and, further up, the town of Canmore. She swooped down just as streetlights flickered on and landed on a leafless apple tree of a yard she knew well.

Warm light splashed onto the ground from inside the house, rich smells seeped from the kitchen, and a man's contagious laughter escaped from the dining room.

Corbalyn cawed and ruffled her feathers.

The girl with the long, black hair lifted her head. She was sitting at the top of the deck stairs and when she saw the crow, she got up and approached the tree slowly.

Corbalyn began to clean her wings.

"Hello, you," the girl said. "Feeling better?"

The crow took no notice and continued her task. Then she pulled at her tail, releasing a feather–her longest and most beautiful one. Holding the feather in her beak, Corbalyn observed the girl for a moment, then let go.

The feather floated to the ground, and the girl picked it up. She held it up to admire it. She looked at the crow with a gleam in her eyes. "A gift," she whispered. "Thank you."

Corbalyn ruffled her feathers once more, then took off into the night.

The girl remained immobile, holding the feather in the palm of her gloved hands.

"Kimi? Diner's ready!" a woman's voice called from inside the house.

The girl didn't move, but when she finally did, she had a smile on her face.

The Alien Skill Series

Book 1
Ben Archer and the Cosmic Fall
https://www.amazon.com/Archer-Cosmic-Fall-Alien-Skill/dp/1984918664

Book 2
Ben Archer and the Alien Skill
https://www.amazon.com/Ben-Archer-Alien-Skill-Book-ebook/dp/B07FS4TK3K

Book 3
Ben Archer and the Moon Paradox
Coming soon

About the Author

Rae Knightly is an indie author who invites the young reader to go on a journey into the imagination, where science-fiction and fantasy blend into the real world. Young heroes are taken on gripping adventures full of discovery and story twists.

Rae Knightly lives in Vancouver with her husband and two children. The breathtaking landscapes of British Columbia have inspired her to write The Alien Skill Series.

Reviews allow indie authors to keep writing the books that you love. Please support the author by posting a short review on Amazon: https://www.amazon.com/Ben-Archer-Alien-Skill-Book-ebook/dp/B07FS4TK3K

To find out about future releases, please refer to:
http://www.raeknightly.com
E-mail: raeknightly@gmail.com
Twitter/Facebook/Instagram: Rae Knightly

Acknowledgments

To Cora, Jonathan and Bob for their valuable insights.
To the people behind the scenes without whose guidance this book would not be what it is.

To you, reader, for taking the time to read
Ben Archer and the Alien Skilll.

Thank you!
Rae Knightly

Made in the USA
San Bernardino, CA
17 May 2020